Victoria Park

Gemma Reeves

ALLEN&UNWIN

Published in hardback in Great Britain in 2021 by Allen & Unwin,
an imprint of Atlantic Books Ltd.

10 9 8 7 6 5 4 3 2 1

A CIP catalogue record for this book is available from the British Library.

Hardback ISBN: 978 1 91163 076 0
Trade paperback ISBN: 978 1 91163 077 7
E-book ISBN: 978 1 76087 406 3

Printed in Great Britain by TJ Books Ltd
Allen & Unwin
An imprint of Atlantic Books Ltd
Ormond House
26–27 Boswell Street
London
WC1N 3JZ

www.allenandunwin.com/uk

For M & T

Contents

October

Smoking Salmon

At the end of Wolfie's garden is a shed he built in the summer of 1951, the same year he turned nineteen and opened the kosher deli next to Victoria Park. He scavenged the timber from a house shattered by the Blitz and laid the roof with red clay tiles prised from the rubble. For sixty-six years he's used it to smoke salmon. It was there when he earned a reputation for the best bagel in Hackney, when he married Mona, when their daughter died, and when he finally retired last year and handed the reins of his business over to his neighbour, Luca.

This morning, Wolfie rose with the first light and went to check on the salmon. He crossed the dewy grass and cracked his shed door open so as not to disturb the dark. He picked up the small flashlight hanging from a rusted nail and used it to illuminate the fish. Suspended from the rafters, they looked like marble sculptures. The walls were seasoned with decades of charred smoke residue, which had turned sticky over time. Its earthy smell reminded him of the huge bonfires they used to light in the park, when he ran around the neighbourhood collecting 'a penny for the guy'.

His method for smoking salmon was known to no one but Mona, and the secrecy added to its appeal. 'Is it beetroot?' customers had asked him. He'd shake his head, 'No, no. Are you crazy?' 'Honey?' they'd venture. He'd laugh. From the day he discovered the right mix of applewood and oak chips, and when Abe the fishmonger started ordering in the wild Loch Duart salmon just for him, Wolfie hadn't changed a thing. He always collected the salmon forty-eight hours before it would be sold, or eaten, and brought them to his shed. He could fit six whole fish in there and carried each one lengthwise like a baby so as not to break the flesh. Then he sharpened his knives, steel on steel ringing out like wedding bells. He sliced away the heads and tails in two confident strokes, then ran the blade along their middles. He held the fillets to the light so they could shine in their silver skins before he removed those too. He then caked their torsos with generous heaps of rock salt and a little molasses, and speared each one with an iron hook.

The salmon for tonight's Shabbas dinner had been curing for ten hours. He examined the crusted bodies hanging from the rafters, and then washed the salt away with a watering can. He lit the woodchips and closed the shed door with a gentle click, like he didn't want to wake them. In twelve hours, the fish would change from pale to deep orange, mirroring the evening trail of the sun as it tucked itself behind the park's ring of beech trees. Then he'd slice it Scandinavian style, vertically, inch thick. The ritual pleased him, the motions and movements familiar – like curving an arm around Mona's body in the night.

He opened the garden gate and headed for the west side of the park. It was a routine Mona had prescribed for him since retirement. 'There's nothing a brisk walk can't fix,' she would say. 'Grump, slump, or fury.' She was right, as she so often was. The air in his lungs inflated his mood; stretching thigh muscles made for a pleasant burn. It was a reminder of his mobility, his good health. The park was almost two hundred years old and he would imagine the tree roots beneath his white plimsolls entwined for decades, spreading out beyond the gates, ambitious and ancient. Black poplar, cider gum, sweet chestnut: they were majestic, yes, but also twisted and stooped – even awkward sometimes, and this made him feel better about his body. The bunions and the lumps and the liver spots. He was ageing and they were ageing, and that was the natural way of things – to grow and degrade.

Grove Road split the park in two, and he followed its length south towards the canal, passing the old boating lake. The island in the middle featured a red Chinese pagoda, flanked by English elms and beeches. Waterfowl, plump from scraps of bread, made abstractions of the weeping willows and yellow laburnum reflected on the water's surface as they swam. Runners lapped the park, friends jogged together in conversation, never short of breath. The dog walkers greeted him. One of the young mums who bought bagels from the deli raised a hand in hello. It was good to see the same people each morning, just as he had when he worked.

Halfway through his usual circuit, he took a seat on his favourite bench and ran his fingers over the faded gold lettering: *Shirley-Ann: the song ended but the melody lingers on.* Such a girlish name, Shirley-Ann. He imagined she'd been a chorus girl – blonde ringlets, blue eyes – but that she'd died young. Left behind a fiancé, maybe. He rubbed his knees. The ache of arthritis was more pronounced in the mornings. He couldn't get used to feeling so aware of his bones.

A middle-aged man yelled at a sheepdog. The women clustered by the rose garden were engrossed in their New Agey thing, all bright leggings and slow arm movements. The turn of their bodies like a baby's mobile, rotating. Whatever it was they were doing, it relaxed him. The sky changed from grey to a pale pink.

In the kitchen, he was greeted by a stack of dirty dishes, half-chopped vegetables, and great piles of garden herbs. Sheets of silver foil and baking paper covered the oak table. Luca always said that the mess shrank the room, defying its high ceiling and the light that flooded through a slanted skylight. But Wolfie liked the kitchen the way it was, the sliding doors the length and width of the back wall opening out on to the garden where he'd watch Mona potter about in soil-caked overalls, humming along to Adele.

A huge pan of water bubbled on the busy hob and Wolfie set a timer to eight minutes. At the sound of the alarm, he drained three dozen eggs and plunged them into a bowl of iced water. Knocking their tops on the granite counter, he peeled each one with deft fingers, leading with the thumb, and deposited the shells in a pile set aside for compost. A mundane job, but he let his thoughts drift. When he ran the deli, he was always tired and irritable by midday. He'd growl at the staff – the salt beef was sliced too thick, the rollmops were tilting in their rows, or he'd curse the shelves buckling under the weight of tinned apricots, sardines, and barrels of pickled herrings. But alone at dawn, Mona still sleeping, he would walk the length of Victoria Park Road, cross the roundabout, and take pleasure in each familiar step of opening the deli. He'd lift the groaning iron shutters, flick the lights, put money in the register, tie his white apron in a determined bow – *Wolfie's* stitched across its breast in royal blue – and welcome the day.

He'd been popular with the customers. They liked his bright, sharp face – the tyranny of red capillaries across the bridge of his nose made him look sunburnt year-round, or as if he had just told a dirty joke. Owning the deli meant he was privy to the neighbourhood gossip. Someone's husband came home blind drunk again, or young so-and-so is in the family way. But Wolfie kept the whisperings to himself.

In those days, he was considered one of the lucky ones. After a rich benefactor befriended him, he'd become his own boss, always certain a pay packet was coming at the end of the week. So he spread his good fortune – even the neighbours he wasn't so keen on were treated to some extra latkes, slipped into a brown paper bag. 'Eat, eat!' he'd insist. 'Stop being so polite. Pick it up with your fingers. It's not biting *you*.' He knew which foods could fix the worst of moods. 'Mrs Klein, you're hankering for a little chicken soup with ginger,' he'd say, rolling the syllables with a faint German accent, too soft for most to notice. 'I feel it in my bones.'

'Lord, yes. That's exactly it,' she'd reply. 'How did you know?'

Cooking helped him to shrink the borders between giving people what they needed and understanding what he needed himself.

He lifted a large mixing bowl from the crowded shelves, leaning a little on tiptoes to reach, and scooped the entire contents of a jar of mayonnaise – made yesterday, slowly, with a generous glug of olive oil – into it. With a fork, he broke the eggs into large chunks until they made a warm orange and cream mess. It had been circulated at synagogue that egg mayonnaise was the new rabbi's favourite bagel. Since then, dozens of challah offerings had been made. But surely none could surpass Wolfie's? If he couldn't impress with his egg mayo then he was finished, though Rabbi Ellensen was an American, and what if they ate theirs with onions or something else meshuge? Well, he would do it his way and the rest was in God's hands.

Wolfie delighted in cooking for guests but nothing gave him more joy than feeding Mona. Mona, who was pencil-slim the day he first saw her whirling around a Mile End dance hall. He'd been too shy to ask her for a date out-right, awed by her golden hair and petticoats which flared beneath her dress as she spun, so he told her to drop by his deli. 'Lemme put some meat on those bones,' he'd said. She came, to his surprise, the very next day and sat at the counter, swinging her tiny feet and hugging her ribs as she guzzled down the plate of prune tzimmes and soused herrings with potato salad that he pushed in front of her.

'I've never tasted anything so good,' she said.

He plonked another dish down, a chicken casserole with latkes that he'd warmed on the stove in the back. 'Try that,' he commanded.

'I'm too full. I couldn't manage another bite!' she pro-tested, laughing.

'Eat! Eat!'

Her murmurs of approval satisfied him and, as he studied her narrow frame, he decided it was up to him to round her out.

He didn't know then that she was a Kindertransport child, too. That her Austrian accent had been beaten out of her by foster parents, or that she'd only been given scraps to eat for years. He'd find all that out only after they were married. But these days Mona toyed with her food, disinterested in the steaming, aromatic plates he served up. He baked her pies with flaky butter crusts and stout-steeped beef shanks, but she would only pick at them, play with the pastry. Not even his chicken soup, with its light nourishing broth and tender meat floating among lokshen, could tempt her. It was as though she'd forgotten the joy that comes from eating. Lately, the outline of her ribcage could be seen through the cotton of her dress. He considered it a personal failure.

He examined a pencil-scrawled schedule, the timings of each dish carefully mapped out. As usual, he'd taken on too much and was expecting all of their closest friends and neighbours for dinner. He couldn't abide a quiet house, hated that there were no abandoned toys strewn across the floor, no washing line full of clothes. The coat rack in particular filled him with a deep melancholy when its pegs were bare. So, he took every opportunity to overcrowd the kitchen table with hungry mouths. With chewing and talking and drinking. With life.

He rolled the challah dough then swiftly turned it into two thick plaits.

Luca's voice called out from the garden and then the back doors slid open. Luca entered with a basket full of chicory, radishes, carrots and horseradish root. He dropped it on the edge of the counter top. 'It's all here,' he said. 'Enough for an army, as usual.' He stooped to kiss Wolfie's cheeks.

Wolfie ruffled Luca's pile of black curls. 'Look at this,' he said, pawing over the produce, checking its quality. 'That alter kocker is redeeming himself. Slowly.'

'Please – no more arguments over tomatoes.'

Wolfie lifted a hand to his balding skull and ran a finger over his overgrown eyebrows, still black when everything else was grey. 'Oy, the principle, son. It's the principle.' He scooped up carrot chunks from the chopping board and dropped them into a pan of water along with gefilte fish.

Luca shook his head and surveyed the kitchen with an expression of amusement. 'Chaos as usual,' he said. 'Elena and the kids want to know what's on the menu.'

Wolfie opened the oven and slid the challah into its depths. 'Well we might have to get creative with what we tell them. Chopped liver. Gefilte fish and beetroot horseradish. Chicken soup. My smoked salmon, of course, then brisket and chicory salad, with Mona's apple strudel to finish.'

'I don't suppose you'll let me help?'

'No, no. All under control.'

Luca took a seat on the brown bar stool and picked up Wolfie's worn cookbook. Bound in green leather, the cover was tacky with old food and marbled oil stains. He flicked through the pages. 'Is there anything you don't deface with stickmen?'

Wolfie laughed. 'Stickmen are the best – they're always pushing or pulling things. If you're going to doodle, at least you can put them to work,' he said. 'Should've kept it pristine, though. A first-edition Florence Greenberg's worth a pretty penny now.'

'Florence who?'

'The other Jewish bible. I've been using her recipes since I learned to boil water. They're like family to me – except without the disappointments!'

Luca smiled, turning the book in his hands.

'How's the new fellow at the deli working out? Any good?' asked Wolfie.

'He's great. Very outgoing. Customers love him. I'll go over for the lunch rush.' Luca leaned in to smell the posy on the table. 'Did Mona pick these? Freddy wants to know if she'd like some help gardening tomorrow?'

'Yes, that'll make her happy. He's a good kid. It's time she ate breakfast. Would you mind bringing her down?'

Luca's heavy tread reverberated on the staircase above. Wolfie scooped a pile of raw liver on to a wooden board and chopped the reddish-brown flesh into chunks before dropping them in a hot iron pan. He filled the sink with warm soapy water and began to clean his knives.

When he looked up a few minutes later and saw the expression on Luca's face, he sighed and took the pan off the heat.

'I've looked everywhere,' Luca said, laying a large hand on Wolfie's shoulders.

'Everywhere?'

Luca nodded.

'Oy gevalt. Oh Mona.'

'She won't have gone far,' Luca said. 'We'll look together. Bet she's at the playground again. We'll find her before the bread is baked.'

There was a long silence as Wolfie turned and opened the fridge, looking into its depths as if his wife might be inside. 'Thank you,' he said softly, 'that'd be a great help.' He closed the door, and then switched off the oven. 'I'll just get my hat.'

Mona refused to wear a watch. She had no interest in the exact time of anything. Instead, she preferred to rely on sun-looking and instinct. When she was a girl in

Austria, just before the train left, her mother slipped her father's gold watch into her hands and told her to keep it safe. At five years old, she hadn't grasped telling the time, but adored the soft brown leather strap, creased and lined from wear, the shine of its gold-rimmed face, the mystery of Roman numerals. All she remembered of her mother now was the outline of her silhouette at the station, shoulders hunched against the wind, the black of her coat. It was her abiding memory of Austria, but it returned to her so often sometimes it felt as though she'd only just left. She still heard the tick of the second hand as it went round and round. The watch was the first thing they took from her when she was sent to the home. So when she left the house this morning, Mona looked up at a blue sky full of low-hanging clouds and figured it was around nine a.m. and Patrice would be about to finish her night shift.

The garden was brimming with pink nerines. She bent down, gathering their spidery petals to her nose, and inhaled. They'd make a wonderful bouquet for her friend. She pulled the thin stems away from the main stalk and took a stray length of brown string from the rose trellis and caught their ends in a tidy bow. She opened the garden gate and crossed the road. She entered the park through Grove Road. Wind whipped up the leaves, their tips turning to rust, and scattered them across the pavement like confetti. It had been raining and the grass seemed replenished, bright and springy, and there was a pleasant earthy smell. She stopped walking, surprised the pens full of guinea pigs, rabbits and wallabies weren't there. Nor was the aviary. Perhaps they'd been taken for cleaning.

The playground was already overrun with shrieking children. How pleasant, to be so free. No over-darned stockings, no hair set in curlers overnight, no lacquered fingernails. How nice to get mud on your shoes! She was still partial to a puddle herself. That was the joy of having your own children, she supposed – a second childhood. Goodness knows the first time round was no picnic. She couldn't wait to have a brood of her own; Henry would make a wonderful father. It was partly why she chose him, of course. And it helped he had a good job at his father's textile factory in Whitechapel. One year of marriage to get themselves on their feet, then they'd start a family.

She passed the Chinese pagoda but it looked different – the paint too red, too new. Where had they found money to spruce it up during rationing? A breeze caught the edges of her yellow dress and she pulled the worn cloth belt around her – it never tied tightly enough. She lusted after the softness of Betty Grable's body, her apple cheeks and plump hips, so wide and appealing. Perhaps that was what it would take for Henry to propose – a little rounding out, softening up. Then he'd see her as the child-rearing kind. The sharp angles of her hips and ribcage were an embarrassment but at least she was a natural blonde and didn't have to fuss with peroxide like Patrice every few weeks. Nothing worse than a sludgy brown parting.

On the east side of the park, a woman sat alone, cross-legged and straight-backed beneath the wide canopy of an ash tree. Her eyes were closed. What on earth could she be doing? Strange – though it was a lovely tree, quite majestic.

Mona sailed on to Old Ford Road with quick, light steps. The sun pushed between cracks of clouds and she sang skipping songs under her breath as the warmth hit her face. *Salt, mustard, vinegar, pepper. Handy-pandy, sugar candy.* Patrice could always skip better than her *and* keep going – even in the dark. Poor Patrice, growing up with a drunk excuse for a father. No wonder she'd ended up in a line of work dealing with dreadful men. And there, look, on a bench were more gutter-minded men, two of them wrapped round one another, elbows and arms interlocking. She tutted as she passed.

She stopped. The shops weren't in the right place. Or was it the right order? She cast around in her mind – what used to be here? Abe's fishmongers? Did he leave Bethnal Green? She kept walking. The pie and mash shop was setting up for lunchtime trade and she looked longingly through the window at its marble tables, its mirrors etched with pictures of eels, seaweed and shells. Had she eaten breakfast? Her stomach felt tight, angry. Probably not. She would walk the long way round past Rinkoffs, buy something warm with cinnamon in it.

Inside the bakery, men and women jostled and pushed one another, shouting orders across the smeary glass counter. She didn't recognize the young man who served her. Was he a Turk? He really should have been wearing a hat to cover all that hair. She pointed at a cinnamon swirl.

'Where's Clive?' she asked, taking the paper-wrapped bun from his large hairy hands.

'Who?'

'Clive. The owner.'

'I don't know who that is, lady.'

'Well you should know who your—'

'That'll be two twenty.'

'What's that?'

'Two pounds twenty.'

She laughed. 'You making fun of me? That's not the price. What do I owe you?' She laid her posy on the counter and felt about in the pockets of her dress. 'Oh. I – I don't have any money on me.'

'You gotta be kidding.' He shook his head. 'Tell you what, lady, I'm too busy for this – it's on me.'

'It is? Well thank—'

The man turned to the next customer.

'Oh,' she said, then bit into the flaky Danish. She savoured the flavour, letting the rich butter pastry go soggy in her mouth as she sucked the cinnamon.

'Mona? What you doing here, lovely?'

The voice had an accent she couldn't place. When a hand was laid on her shoulder she spun round. A concerned-looking woman was staring at her. She had olive skin, smooth and bright, and her eyes crinkled at the corners.

'Who are you?' Mona asked.

The woman smiled. 'It's me: Veronica.'

She looked hard at the woman. 'I – I don't know any Veronica.'

'I clean your house every Monday, Mona. Lovely, aren't you cold in that summer dress?'

'You're confused,' Mona said, 'and I'm afraid you're making me late.' She glanced at the woman again, and then left the bakery.

Outside, the whine of cranes and juddering drills offended her. So many men with strange hats and huge plastic glasses. People were speaking to each other at ear-splitting volume. She looked at the street ahead, wondering what brought her here. 'What are you staring at?' she asked a passing young girl who didn't appear to hear her.

She kept walking. Strange music blared from food stalls in Whitechapel market. She couldn't isolate the different sounds and they stung and jolted her. The high street was busier than she'd ever seen it; it was wild with colour. She sneezed several times, something peppery teasing her nose. A breeze of recognition fluttered over her and she remembered Cable Street and Patrice's shift. She drifted in its direction, following the narrow road slowly but the movement of people around her was rapid. Light pulsed. More strange music. She reached a junction and was mesmerized by the tallness of trees, towers of green glass. Everything reaching up, up, up.

Wolfie walked with pronounced steps as if treading on sand not pavement. It wasn't that he didn't want to hurry, but maybe if his pace could be measured, then the gnawing thrum inside him might quieten too. He'd noticed Luca's usual long gait had slowed to half-time and now there was a prick of embarrassment along with a growing sense of panic. They'd checked the playground and across the long stretch of Cambridge Heath. He was worried about the road, the rush of traffic, the speed of all those young cyclists, weaving through cars. And what if she stumbled? One trip is all it would— Just one.

The sunlight was bouncing off the concrete now. He rolled back his shirtsleeves and found his watch read midday – they left the house thirty minutes ago. Church bells pealed in the distance and he realized Luca was asking a question.

'The first time she wandered off she made it as far as Lea Valley,' Wolfie replied. 'She used to play around the marshes when she was a girl. Then it was the museum on Cambridge Heath Road, then Meath Gardens on Roman Road, though it was called Green Street in those days. She used to walk all over Hackney back then.'

'If Lydia went further than the park I'd have a fit!'

'It was a different time.' Wolfie shrugged. He tilted his head up to the sky and let the first real warmth of the day roll across his face. He closed his eyes, the past breaking open in him and with it a brief betrayal of happiness. 'There wasn't any fear of strangers. We all knew each other. No adults fussed unless you didn't show up for mealtimes – then you'd get the belt if your dinner went cold. Though it was never much more than bread and dripping.' He opened his eyes and took in the press of the crowd around Bethnal Green tube station. The street swelled with people – so many more than when he and Mona were young, when Bethnal was considered a Jewish ghetto. 'You should have seen Mona in those days,' he said. 'Her hair was like gold before it turned silver.'

There was a buzzing in Wolfie's pocket, which was alarming until he remembered the present Luca gave him for his birthday. He pulled out the small black phone.

'Luca, I don't have my reading glasses.' He handed it over. 'What does it say?'

'From Veronica,' Luca said. 'She just saw Mona at Rinkoffs but Mona didn't recognize her.'

'Af tsores. How could she not know Veronica?' Wolfie murmured. 'Rinkoffs was where she used to stop off on the way to see Patrice.'

'Who?'

'Her best friend when she was young. She died years ago.'

Luca paused. 'Do you think maybe it's time?'

'Not you as well. It's not up for discussion.'

'She's putting herself in more and more danger.'

'This isn't danger. It's broad daylight. She's just confused. No more of this, OK?'

Luca frowned and fell quiet. As they rounded the corner on to Whitechapel High Street, the passing snippets of conversation grew louder, younger and more urgent. The street was littered with the pulp of dropped tomatoes, stray chillies, coriander leaves. Shouts of the market-stall men added to the clamour. It sounded like music, the sustained notes of an unknown language. They passed students loitering outside the hospital college, their dizzying array of styles recognizable from each decade he'd lived through. The stream of whizzing bicycles unsettled him.

'Slow down,' Wolfie muttered to the back of their heads.

'Freddy wants one of those fixed-gear bikes. But over

my dead body is he going to cycle through London with no brakes.' Luca stepped aside to avoid a young family as they spilled out of a new block of flats.

'How I hate those places,' Wolfie said, pointing at a recently opened Tesco Metro. 'Sad aisles full of pre-chopped veg and microwave meals. So lonely.'

'I can see her,' Luca said, his voice breathy with relief. 'Who's she talking to?'

Wolfie followed Luca's gaze and saw a flash of bright yellow. Mona hadn't worn that dress in a long time. He remembered the day she bought it – ten, twelve years ago? Monty had driven them down to Brighton in his old green Astra. Mona trawled through the packed rails in the Lanes, enamoured with the brightly coloured clothes. When she yanked aside the changing-room curtain to show him, she looked like an after-image of the sun – a vision burned on his retina. She'd bought a necklace that day too, he recalled, though lost it soon after. It had a clasp that wouldn't quite catch.

Across the street now, Mona was gesturing wildly to a shopkeeper, a shadow of hair under her exposed arms. He watched her for a long time, or what seemed like a long time, perhaps it was only a few seconds, and he saw his life in a flickering reel behind him with nothing in front.

'Maybe she thinks he's Patrice's pimp,' Wolfie said. 'A lot of her friends from the children's home ended up prostitutes.'

Luca was silent and took Wolfie's arm, and they walked to where Mona was arguing loudly with a Bengali man.

'Mona, altz iz gut,' Wolfie said. 'Come on, my darling, let's go home. You'll feel better there.' He grasped the pointed end of her elbow with his hand and guided her away.

'Where's Patrice? Tell this man. You must do something!'

He wanted to do something but didn't know what, so he embraced her, put his face in her hair, breathed in the familiar scent of camomile shampoo, and felt the urgency of her heartbeat. She pulled away abruptly and yelled at him only inches from his face and her breath was sweet like cinnamon.

The kitchen was warm with bodies crowded around the oak table, its sliding extensions pulled out with a snap and draped in the lace Shabbas tablecloth moments before his guests arrived. Wolfie had set the table with the good china and crystal glasses with red paper napkins folded inside, their gold edges fanned out. He lit the long-stemmed Shabbas candles before sunset to honour the Torah's commandments to guard and remember, one of the few traditions he still adhered to, and now the wavy flames cast his friends and neighbours in a flattering glow. The aroma of baked bread, smoked salmon, and the spice of patchouli – Monty's preferred cologne – mingled in the air. Everyone had brought flowers, except Rabbi Ellensen who'd greeted him with a jar of home-made blackberry jam. He'd run out of vases and didn't know where Mona kept the rest.

He sat at the head of the table, masterminding the consumption by murmuring, 'Eat, eat,' until soon the eating and talking were no longer distinct. Chomping, agreeing, chewing, interrupting, cutting, scraping. Sounds of satisfaction. The clang of porcelain dentures on silverware.

'Wonderful egg mayonnaise, Wolfie,' Rabbi Ellensen said. She kissed the crumbs from her fingers.

He smiled back at her. She looked younger up close than she did standing on the synagogue's small stage. She was the first female rabbi he'd ever met, and under forty too. She'd moved from California with her husband for his job, she'd told him. They'd been married fifteen years, which felt like child's play.

There were murmurs of agreement about the mayonnaise. It would have all been perfect if Mona hadn't been upstairs, sleeping. But the compliments fell flat, the conversation washing over him. He'd answer, 'That's right, that's right,' only to find that no question had been asked. He picked at a liver cracker. Perhaps a long sleep might break Mona's cycle; maybe she'd even wake up hungry. He didn't want to disturb her but longed to put a hand on her knee under the table, for the rabbi to meet her properly. Hosting the rabbi for Shabbas was a much-coveted spot, and her attendance today had been booked months in advance. She'd led a wonderful Kiddush, complimented the beautiful textiles Mona had stitched to cover the challah when the wine was blessed. When the rabbi tore the bread to pass around the table, she spoke softly of the value of shalom bayit, peace in the home, and he'd had to bow his head.

He observed the crowded dinner table, full of friends and neighbours and their children, the family that he and Mona had made for themselves, and he felt like a witness – not a participant.

Monty caught his gaze. 'Tell us about the Italian lessons, Wolfie,' he said.

'Well, apart from being the oldest person at college by about forty years, it's all very enjoyable,' he replied. 'I want to take Mona to Florence, order fave e cicoria, riso and patate e cozze with a perfect accent. Like a second honeymoon of sorts.'

Luca and Elena praised his pronunciation but he caught the look of surprise they shared. He felt a kick of annoyance.

'We never went on a honeymoon,' Elena said.

'Neither did we, come to think of it,' Wolfie replied. 'It was still rationing time.'

'Imagine the shopping in Florence,' Monty said. 'Mona is the perfect Italian size. And you could do with some dapper clothes.'

Wolfie smiled. 'I'll leave that to you, my friend.' He stood and tapped a fork against the edge of his wine glass. 'Firstly, everyone please fill your glasses, for a day without wine is like a day without sunshine.' He paused to let the Beaujolais pass around the table. 'I want to thank you all for joining us on this Shabbas, particularly Rabbi Ellensen who we welcome into our community and who I'm honoured will be blessing Mona and I at our sixty-fifth wedding anniversary in the new year.'

The room resounded with the clink of crystal.

'Mona and I have been fortunate enough to witness the many comings and goings of this neighbourhood, and though there are some who have sadly passed on, our circle is always growing. It's a shame Mona's not feeling well today because nothing makes her happier than celebrating Shabbas with the people she loves. So,' Wolfie raised his glass once more, 'to you all and to new beginnings.'

'No – to you and Mona,' Monty said, 'our favourite cantankerous fools. We love you.'

Wolfie performed a little bow. He took a long drink of wine, then went to the oven and brought a tray of brisket back to the table. Its flesh crumbled as he portioned it out. His guests emitted throaty hums of appreciation as it was passed down. He watched as Elena spooned some of the meat juices from the serving platter on to Freddy's plate. The boy kept his head down low, close to the dish, and nodded a little in thanks as he shovelled food into his mouth, slurping. Elena smiled a small smile as he ate before rolling the sleeves of her black cardigan and serving herself. Luca was opposite, looking after Lydia. Wolfie realized he hadn't heard husband and wife say a single word to one another all evening, save for a polite request to pass the horseradish.

'Do you have to keep your phone on the table, Freddy?' Luca asked his son.

'What's all this? Where's Henry?' Mona's small frame appeared in the doorway. Her hair was mussed from sleep, her face pale against the yellow dress, rippled now with creases.

'Who's Henry, Aunt Mona?' Lydia asked, abandoning the panda doodle that had begun to take shape on her napkin.

'My sweetheart, of course. Who are you?'

Freddy looked up from his plate and turned to Elena. Monty lowered his head and the warmth of the brisket steamed the lenses of his tortoiseshell glasses. Wolfie saw in the rabbi's face a slackening, a moment of lost composure, though she recovered quickly.

'Wolfie, perhaps Mona needs some more rest,' Luca said.

'Or dinner?' Freddy offered.

'Yes, both, I think,' Wolfie said. 'Come, my darling, let's take this brisket upstairs.' He excused himself from the table, picked up his plate, and with a wave he instructed the eating to continue.

He clasped his wife's small hand and together they climbed the stairs to their bedroom. The room was stuffy and with great effort he pushed up the sash window and let in the cool evening air. He stood for a moment and looked out at the silhouetted beech trees and the park beyond. When he turned, Mona had already slipped beneath the blue floral sheets, their pattern chosen after an agonizing twenty-minute deliberation at last year's John Lewis Christmas sale. He remembered her fussing over the greens and pinks, lifting one set out after another and inspecting their cloth. How infuriating he'd found her interest in thread count, barking at her to hurry up and choose – it was only linen. He pulled the cord of the bedside lamp and Mona's face submerged in the shadows, her silver hair spread across the pillow, and as he looked at her confused, worn-out expression, he wished furiously to go back to that moment and tell her to buy all of them.

November

Tenderly

The trick to a successful break-in was to either think really small or really big. It was the medium-sized jobs that messed you up – this was something Daniel had learned from Mum. Also, for the conscience, only take from those who have too much, or things that can easily be replaced. He'd got that one off Robin Hood, and it kind of held up in church, too, if you thought about it long enough.

He had two hours before Nan got home from the Westfield where she worked the make-up counters. She was sixty-six but could pass for Mum's age, and no one and nothing was more important to her than the Good Lord. She quoted Him as she plaited the twins' hair in the mornings, she praised Him when she got the right answer on her game shows, and daily she thanked Him for His love and kindness for their telly – its glorious forty-six inches, flat screen and HD sharpness. It was the envy of Nan's church friends, her sewing circle, and – most importantly – their whole block of flats. It had belonged to Mum (though it was anyone's guess where she'd got it) and was the one spoil of her Devious and Wicked Ways to which Nan had turned a blind eye. It was under the care of this TV that he left his sisters, zombified by Christmas cartoons. Time to do one quick job and be back to say grace at dinner. He stuffed the last chip in his mouth – no one can do a break-in on an empty stomach – and set off for Monty's house.

At this time of year six p.m. looked like the middle of the night and Bethnal Green Road was heaving. He walked to the beat of honks and the thump-thud-thud of car stereos. Normally he'd cycle but some prick had swiped his bike's saddle when it was locked up outside Tesco the other day. He missed flying through STOP signs, taking corners like they belonged to him, legs working double-time, the ones Mum said kicked her non-stop in the womb, dying to get out.

Buses waded through rush hour, emptying out a few people at each stop, gaining some in return. Their faces were flat and jaded through the misted windows, blue LED lights lending them a ghoulish glow. He thought of Nan, how she flopped on the couch when she got in, zoning-out to presenters with gleaming teeth and Tango skin.

In front of the buses was a trail of black cabs. He stared down the drivers. Were they wondering what was in his backpack? Or checking out his Levi's and the black parka that bulked out his skinny frame? – he'd done a good job stitching up the cigarette burn. It was bitter out, but he didn't pull up the hood. Bettie had told their class that morning: *Don't let them twist the word youth like it's a dirty word, like it doesn't mean just young any more.*

Supermarket, betting shop, nail salon, phone repair stand on an endless loop. The market stretched along the main road and he dodged the men breaking down their stalls, ladders and poles flung over shoulders. Rolling rotten fruit. They yelled at each other in a language he didn't understand, offered him calling cards to ring home for 1p a minute, but he said, 'No, mate – home's right here.' For a few hundred yards every brick wall had NAT HAS HERPES tagged in bright white paint. He shook his head at the kids selling weed; he only smoked Lemon Haze – none of that paranoia shit they were flogging.

At the traffic lights, bottle caps and broken glass cracked beneath his black Nikes. The lifetime drinkers were huddled in a smokers' group outside the Salmon and Ball. That pub was as rough as it'd always been, no crab on toast or venison pie there. Those old boys caused trouble when they were tanked. Sometimes he saw them in the kebab shop after last call, mouthing off to the staff, gobs stuffed with doner. The best thing about delivering takeout was dropping off food, and then speeding away. He'd no patience for drunk night-hunger.

It was impossible to walk down Cambridge Heath Road in a straight line. A sleepy-eyed woman tugged at his jacket and asked for 80p for a hostel. She was cracked-out but it was freezing so he slipped her a quid. The City boys were headed to those crazy-priced wine bars down Paradise Row, or the restaurants that only served raw food – what they had against hot grub he'd never know. There were split bags of clothes outside the charity shop. Mismatched kids' shoes made their escape across the street. He hopped over the mess and collided with an Alpha Course weirdo who asked: *Do you ever think about the meaning of life?* Like he didn't have enough of that nonsense from Nan's church loons. If only he could tell them he'd been free of God since he was ten. At church one Sunday, a kid had whispered that if you didn't finish the Lord's Prayer it wiped out the meaning. From then on, he'd only mouthed the word *Amen* during service – going against God with his silence, not his words.

The constant streaking blue lights of the police, or an ambulance, bounced from shop window to window so there was no telling which direction they were coming from. But the sirens quietened the closer he got to the park. The air was different round there, like more of it got into your lungs. In Bethnal Green it felt like exhaust fumes were pumped around in an endless spin like one of them Dysons Nan harped on about. A cute girl passed by, backside vibrating in a lilac tracksuit. He loved the trend for peach-shaped bums. Girls like that must do a hundred squats a day or something. Her long nails were shaped like coffin lids.

He entered Vicky Park through the east gate. Moonlight cast leaf patterns on the pavement. It was quiet – but not the good kind, more like the sort which let in noisy thoughts. Usually it was mad busy with cyclists and runners – even at night – but it looked like no one was taking any chances after the acid attack yesterday. The place was still sectioned off with police tape. It didn't freak him out but the silence was weird. At school, they'd said you could see parts of the guy's face where they'd melted into the pavement. He was only a couple of years older. What would you have to do to someone to have acid thrown at you? He longed to put in headphones but had to stay alert. Eyes and ears open, Mum would say. Be prepared for anything.

Music helped when he zipped round the houses doing deliveries. He got Employee of the Month for being so speedy – Nan's face when he showed the certificate was a picture. It was amazing how many people ordered take-away from the Italian. Pizza, he understood. But breaded veal? Baked aubergine? Even pasta – like they hadn't got the time to boil water and drop the stuff in. This was how he'd met Monty – the man with a military routine. He ordered a margarita pizza or penne arrabbiata at seven p.m, six nights a week, except for Fridays when he had dinner with his friends across the park. Each time Monty opened the door he said, 'Evening, young Daniel,' bowed a little and dipped his old-fashioned hat. His dentures didn't fit right so he whistled softly as he spoke. He always wore a three-piece suit with a cravat at the neck. He said that's what you wear if you're a Savile Row tailor – it's a lifestyle, not a job. And for an old guy, Monty looked fresh. Daniel liked him, so today he was only going to nick some patterns and fabric to make shirts. Nan had shown him how to lay out the fabric, draw on the pattern, cut and pin the pieces to be sewn together along the seams with her Singer. You had to suss out the right tension to stop the fabric puckering or breaking, the appropriate length of stitch. All he wanted was to know what it felt like to wear something different every day.

Sharp wind shot up the gaps between his jeans and socks. A homeless guy was using a bin as a toilet – he didn't seem to care about the acid attacker on the loose either.

Daniel came out the other side of the park and turned on to Monty's street. This was the bit he loved the most: target in sight, body pulsing like a live wire. The anticipation was like a hundred birthdays all at once. Monty told him that when he was a kid Vicky Park was known as the People's Park. Some lord designed it after people working in East End factories and living in cheap overcrowded houses started dying from the shitty conditions. Queen Victoria was told about the need for fresh air and green space, gave the royal nod, and the park was named for her.

Monty thought the real reason they built it was because the rich didn't want the working classes in Hyde Park, so gave them one of their own. Looking about now, it was hard to believe anyone poor had ever lived here. Shaggy tree roots broke through the concrete, and the bushes and vines rich people loved to plant outside their houses bulged along brick walls. Pink recycling bins, electric-car charging stations, chimneys smoking. A few houses had put up Christmas trees – gold glinting in the windows, baubles reflecting the telly.

Monty's house was painted pale grey with thick black gloss on the front door, a gold-rimmed letter box and a heavy brass knocker the shape of a lion's head. The old man had an eye for detail. The kitchen window was always left open a crack. Daniel did a quick check to see if anyone was about. No evening dog walkers, no one on their way to the pub on the corner, just a few cars whose drivers didn't glance in his direction. He guessed the last of the posh kids had finished their violin lessons or whatever they did after school and were back home now, waiting for tea. He slipped on his gloves. They were smooth black suede – last year's Christmas present from Nan.

He pulled himself up on to the kitchen windowsill. Crouched and pushed. The window was harder to budge from the outside than he'd thought. The muscles in his arms burned until finally it gave a few inches. He wedged his backpack in first, and then scrambled through the gap. Times like these he was thankful to be skinny. *Amen to the Good Lord*, Nan would say. *Praise Him for your long thin body.*

He tumbled in a heap on to the kitchen's tiled floor. Even through his jeans it felt like ice. Inside smelled of furniture polish, or like when you open a new box of trainers. He brushed himself down and pulled the window to a crack again. It took a minute for his eyes to adjust to the darkness, broken only by slivers of street light coming through the window blinds, turning everything blue-black. The quiet of the house was something you could sink into, like swimming underwater. You could sleep through the whole night here – no drunken yells from the street below. Or the loud on-a-mission exchanges of crackheads on the corner, discussing who's serving and where to pick up.

He switched on his phone's torch and carefully swung its beam of light around the room. The house was smaller than he'd thought – though Monty had a massive kitchen table for someone who ordered food for one. He checked the fridge: mustard, a stick of butter, eight cans of cherry cola. This place was definitely a bachelor pad, an extension of his suits. Clearly no female about. It was hard to imagine. Daniel's home was full of women; his teachers at school were women; his boss at the Italian was a woman. His head echoed with female voices. At night, his eyelids danced with the biro-scrawls of Mum's letters.

In the hallway was a crystal chandelier and the walls were covered in purple and gold paper like something out of that *Downton Abbey* Nan was addicted to. Four portraits hung in a row. Thick oily brushstrokes, globs of paint pushed around to make fleshy distorted features. He wondered if the acid boy's skin dripped off in the same way. Close up he saw that the wallpaper was peeling and damp crept along the ceiling like at home.

The living room was bursting with books, dark leather spines, heavy-looking, like Nan's Bible when she waved it around threatening to whack him on the backside. They looked nothing like the ones Bettie gave him at school – thin paperbacks that ripped as soon as he shoved them in his bag. In the corner was an ancient telly, the kind people watched the moon landing on in films. He settled into a velvet armchair. It was the most comfortable thing he'd ever sat in. If he owned this chair, it would be difficult to leave the house. Maybe this was where Monty actually ate dinner, sinking into its soft cushion, the takeout box on his knees, some old record spinning, book in hand. Along one wall was a mirrored drinks cabinet; bottles reflected to look infinite, and wine with the cork half stuffed back in. A record player's needle rested in the vinyl groove, cigar stubs spilled from an ashtray balanced on the arm of the sofa. The whole room felt suspended like it was lying in wait for its owner to come back.

He picked up a framed black and white photo of a young man in a tuxedo. It was impossible to tell whether it was Monty or not. It was next to a book called *Gentlemen of Bacongo*. He remembered reading something about these guys online. Sapeurs, they were called – taste makers. They wore fine threads in war-broken villages. He had a lot of respect for that kind of self-image. Monty had good taste. He'd borrow the book for a while.

In the hallway, the banister was polished and shining and he resisted the urge to run up and slide down. Instead, he took the creaky stairs one at a time and pushed open what he figured was the bedroom door, sticking his head in first like someone might be there. Monty had done a good job with the place. Silky red curtains, red wallpaper too, but a deeper shade with mad swirling patterns. It suited the lingering peppery incense scent he must've picked up from the guys at the market. A huge bed dominated the room and looked like something Santa would fly in, all dark wood and curling frame, a fur blanket and leather headboard. He was careful not to stand in front of the window. The old-fashioned street lamp outside lit up the wall of wardrobes. He flung open the wooden doors and there were Monty's suits, an army of them, two rows deep and swaying from the sudden intrusion. The colours were wild. He took off a glove and ran his hands along the line of fabrics. Some were soft to touch, others sandpaper-rough. Brown checks, fire-red tartan, deep blues. Flashy lining, the kind of get-up no one could ignore you in.

He slipped a pinstripe jacket from its wooden hanger – it would look good with jeans and a white T-shirt – and put it on. He twisted and turned in a large oval mirror, but it hung awkwardly from his shoulders. It'd been made to button up over a big belly. The next three jackets were all hopeless too. The shirts would be too big as well, but he took one as an example to follow.

Inside the chest of drawers were bow ties, braces, cuff-links with polished stones, carefully folded squares of silk. He picked up a yellow one – it reminded him of summer holidays, not the ones Nan took them on to Southend, but the kind you saw on TV ads with sandy beaches, a burning sun, and coconuts. No wonder Monty always had a smile on his face when he opened the front door – he was walking around like he was in Bermuda. Daniel tucked the square in his jeans pocket, and then rooted around to find a pair of socks to match. He nabbed ones with tiny checks on them – they'd be perfect with his white Adidas.

In the small room next door, pattern books were scattered across a desk. He took three from the pile, making a silent promise to return them in a couple of weeks. A black box with an embossed gold elephant on the lid looked just like the one he kept weed in. Inside were three pairs of sewing scissors and reels of thread. Discovering where Monty kept his fabric proved trickier. He sent up dust clouds searching leather boxes stacked under the desk. Invoices, bills, black and white photos of people who looked like they hated having their picture taken. He straightened and turned to carry on his search and that was when he saw Monty, fast asleep in an armchair.

Everything went wavy.

His knees bunched together. He shook. 'You're fine,' he whispered to himself. 'You've got this. All you need to do is back away and fly down those stairs and out the front door.' But he'd been banging around, slamming drawers, nowhere near as careful as usual. So why hadn't Monty woken up? He took a step closer. It was the first time he'd ever seen Monty without a hat and he looked much older with his grey hair uncombed. His skin was pale yellow – like when you clench your knuckles together until all the colour disappears. And there was a funny smell, like butter that'd been left out in the sun.

And that's when he knew.

Shit, shit, shit. He couldn't swallow and his teeth ached like he'd had three cans of Coke. Monty. Jesus. Why today? He realized his palm was clamped to his cheek. The suede smelled like coins long-buried in a jacket pocket. He let his hand fall back to his side. Now what? It was gross but he went closer. Monty's face seemed soft, not stiff like he would have thought. The skin was loose around his bones, slack, and there was a shadow of grey stubble. He leaned forward, breath held, daring himself to touch Monty's shoulder. It was warm. For a moment he wanted to throw his arms around him.

He stood back. Monty was slumped right down in the chair. His neck was the colour of a fresh bruise. Daniel's eyes wandered down. Crisp white shirt, brown waistcoat. And that's when he saw the porn mag, pages creased where it had fallen. Two greasy tanned guys posing with oily hands all over each other stared back up at him. Jesus. He should've figured Monty was a gay. The guys' abs were good, though, he'd give them that.

He looked back at Monty and that's when he saw the purple tip of his cock poking out the zipper of his tweed trousers. Dear God. Fucking hell. He had to get outta there fast but he wasn't a brute, he wouldn't just leg it; it wasn't decent to leave an old man like that. So he held his breath, squeezed his nose shut, and pulled the silk handkerchief from Monty's waistcoat pocket and laid it across his lap. He grabbed the porno, stuffed it in his backpack so he could bin it on the way home – then fled.

Outside, he sucked on the sweet air and tried to slow his heartbeat. The sky was heavy and swollen and the lightness of the first drops was shocking at first – he was expecting a sheet of rain to shatter above him like glass. He stayed by the house for a second, letting the downpour streak through his hair, cool his skin, and then he burst into a run.

Raindrops dripped from spindly branches, sliding down thick trunks, coating the grass. His steps synched with the tip-tip-tip of rain piercing pond water with tiny pricks, and he whirled round the bends, out of the park and on to Cambridge Heath Road, legs stretched out like they were a separate part of him, trying to leap over the cracks in the pavement, weaving through the crowds of workers headed for the nearest pint. Phone-repair stand, nail salon, betting shop, supermarket. From the slap and suck-suck sound of his trainers as they pounded the pavement, he knew dirty puddle water was splashing his jeans.

Running like this, he could almost forget where he was going. It was addictive, that feeling of your body moving just outside of your control. Mum used to run every morning after dropping the twins off at school. He'd seen her sometimes round Weavers Fields when he bunked off. She was good, had her technique down – arms pumping forward, back straight, head erect. He had her stamina, that's what it was, the thing they shared. Stubbornness too. It didn't seem fair, the way everything was racing on without her now. He couldn't forget how he had frozen in that moment when the police came to their door. The look of pure apology on her face, how both hands clutched the pocket of her sweatshirt like it was an emergency brake.

The rain doubled its efforts like the sky was weeping and he whispered, 'Monty, is that you, man? Are you mad?' And then – fuck – he remembered he didn't even get the fabric – the most important bit.

He slowed to a jog. The rain dripped into his eyes so he pulled up his hood. Breath ragged, chest heaving. And as he stepped on to his street, he swore he could feel it vibrating with Nan's hymns, the swell and ache of the full voice she pushed out from her chest. It made her seem so vital, so large, even though she was only five two and he'd been towering over her since he could remember. And that voice, it wasn't sweet – it was fire. And she sang of fire, of heaven and hell. It made him more afraid of her than any God.

He raced up the breezeblock stairway, fourth floor, the letter box that never quite snapped shut, turned the key – plastic Christmas tree already in the corner, flashing lights, no baubles, his sisters pirouetting across the kitchen. Nan singing the GoCompare jingle, a clattering

of plates and glasses, metal spoon against casserole pot
– and he slid into his seat at the top of the table, bowed
his head, and felt the words slip automatically from his
mouth: *Our Good Lord, thank you for the food before
us, the family and friends beside us and the love between
us*, and – for the first time in a long time – he let himself
say the word *Amen*.

December

Sitting

The pain between Mia's legs was indeterminate. Not quite a dull ache. Not quite sharp or searing. The ultrasound probe was too wide, too enquiring. The jelly cold and slick. In the left-hand corner of the ceiling was a charcoal-like smear. She stared at it.

'Try to relax, you're squeezing out the speculum,' Dr Richards said. He looked up at her with a frown.

'Mmhmm,' she replied.

She was on step four: Progress Evaluation. Dr Richards' hands pressed down on her lower stomach. She thought about: the Thanksgiving parade the year she lived in Manhattan; the blur of a white vinyl an ex-girlfriend played on repeat; the time her cat leaped from the dresser to the wardrobe and actually made it.

This is how you're going to make a baby, she reminded herself. A baby. For thirty years, her body had been functional and pleasantly average. Breasts at twelve years old.

Period at thirteen. She'd never broken a bone. The only time spent in hospital was for an appendectomy which took the half hour it should have done – no post-op complications. She considered what she'd pay to return to her former nonchalance, to not take her resting temperature each morning, or study her knickers for the clear sticky discharge that indicated an egg had dropped. Injections, pills, pessaries, powders and tinctures. A puffy, bruised belly. It was not the process she'd imagined. And then she thought about how she and Bettie were broke. Minus-money. She squirmed on the bed.

'OK, Mia.' Dr Richards pulled out the speculum. 'You can sit up and get dressed.'

She exhaled. The lubricant pooled on to the blue paper cloth beneath her. Dr Richards drew the curtain around the bed.

Mia and Bettie had been putting money aside to get on the property ladder for two years. Now they'd blown their fifteen thousand pounds deposit on IVF. But Mia didn't really care about being a home-owner; she cared about being a mother. She'd been sucker-punched by a desire to have a baby shortly after her twenty-seventh birthday. At the time, she had no secure income, no career-path, lived in a house with five other artists and could put away two grams of cocaine on a weekend. The maternal yearning was inconvenient and insistent. It grew and grew, as physical as any high, as any malady. Bettie, on the other hand, had more than her fill of kids at the Pupil Referral Unit, working with teenagers. She would leave a café if anyone under the age of sixteen walked in.

Bettie had finally come around to the idea last spring. Mia put it down to a combination of three things. The immersion tactic: at weekends, she filled their flat with their straight friends' kids, pacified by warm milk and the songs she sang for hours at a time. *Aren't they gorgeous when they're sleeping?* Seasonal help from Spring herself: voluptuous trees, buds breaking open, cumulus clouds, seventeen-degree days. *The possibility of new things growing.* And then the tumour in Mia's breast, the weeks of worry, the overwhelming relief when they found it was benign. *You know I'd do anything for you.*

Reciprocal IVF wasn't available on the NHS and Mia wanted Bettie to be part of the process. She wanted their child to have Bettie's nose, or her cheekbones – even the know-it-all look in her eyes. So they'd gone to Dr Ali. He was the Fertility Whisperer, possessor of a triumphant birth rate. With him they blew three and a half grand the week before Bettie's fortieth birthday only to find out her eggs weren't viable.

Mia slipped off the table and rubbed her legs. They were pink and goosefleshed. Her whole body felt distorted. Her clothes were in a pile on a blue plastic chair. She shed her gown, rolled opaque black tights over her feet, jiggled them up and across her hips, then tugged a cream wool dress over her head. It caught in her gold bracelets and she swore quietly.

'All right in there?' Dr Richards asked.

She left the soiled tissue on the bed, pulled the curtain aside and took a seat opposite Dr Richards. She crossed and then uncrossed her legs. Crossed then uncrossed her ankles. Dr Richards stared into his computer screen. It was large and square and heavy-backed, the shape a kid would draw.

'You're doing well,' he said. 'We know you're a great candidate. You've got good stock.'

She half-expected him to stroke her nose, offer her a sugar cube. Being thirty seemed to ingratiate her to reproductive endocrinologists. Only a lesbian, she could see them thinking, relief flashing across their faces as they weighed up the relative thickness of her uterine walls, healthy oestrogen levels, the satisfactory width of her fallopian tubes.

'You're perfectly positioned for harvesting,' he continued.

She let out her breath.

'One final hormone injection to help the eggs mature. Timing is everything so we'll take them within twelve hours of ovulation. Then implantation,' he said, finally looking away from the computer and resting his hands on the desk. His fingers were enticingly plump, with thick wide thumbs. She ached to draw them, exaggerate the sweet fat of the knuckles. He gave her a small smile, scratched his cheek. He wasn't as warm as Dr Ali, but he hadn't asked why Bettie wasn't with her today and for that she could have kissed his whiskery mouth. She grinned back at Dr Richards. She didn't know how to express her relief.

'The sperm is on its way, yes?' he asked.

She nodded. 'Just in time for Christmas.'

They'd chosen their sperm the previous week. She'd tried to make it fun, playful. For dinner she'd roasted butternut squash, carving the orange flesh into replicas of the male member, the veins hyper-realistic, adding broccoli for a pubic flourish, then whipped feta the magic – missing – ingredient. This had not gone down well.

'It was hard to choose,' she said. 'At the Danish sperm supermarket, I mean. That's what we call it. A big soup of possibility.'

She and Bettie had stared into the laptop screen, scrolling through photographs of babies and toddlers held by proud parents. Oversized heads matted with hair, faces that seemed to spill out, lacking boundaries, bodies like pudding. It was an assault of success stories.

'The language of the website was… tricky. Bettie took great offence to being addressed as *the childless*. They used that phrase on every page. It stings, you know? Like couples without kids are a collective noun.'

Dr Richards emitted what he must have assumed to be a sympathetic noise.

'Deciding whether we wanted anonymous or non-anonymous was difficult. Bettie fixated on how non-anonymous isn't the right word – classic English teacher, right? Apparently hetero couples prefer anonymity to protect the integrity of the father figure but the rest of us don't mind. Such sweeping statements are bullshit.'

Dr Richards raised his eyebrows. His gaze wandered momentarily and sought out the wall clock she knew was above her head.

She and Bettie had made an account and read the lengthy health information about the donors and their extended families, the psychometric profiles. They listened to voice recordings about their values and interests. They all seemed to have names that her tongue could really curl around. Aldrino, Malthe, Villum. They scrolled and scrolled, a cool space on her thigh where Bettie's hand normally rested.

'Anyway, we ended up going with the one who had the best track record of producing children,' she said. 'Like, fifty kids. Imagine that. Fifty little yous out there in the world.'

It had been Bettie who'd settled on their donor, despite the lingering doubts Mia knew Bettie was still wrestling with. Bettie said they should ignore physical attributes and intelligence claims. They should just focus on it *working*. Mia had kissed the whole of her face, inhaling the sour-melon tang of cheap white wine. She really missed drinking.

They ended the night with a hormone shot in Mia's backside. 'Remember when we used to fuck in bathrooms at parties,' Bettie said.

It was ten a.m. by the time she left the doctor's office. The morning grog had been snuffed out by bright but bitter sun. Street flotsam whipped up into the air – crisp packets, crisped leaves. It took a moment to readjust. Her body raced with hormones. People swirled around her, charging across the road, ignoring the benevolent command of traffic lights. Cars beeped, sirens wailed.

She looked up at the lamp posts strung with elegant Christmas lights, their colours muted until evening when they'd burst into reds and blues and golds. Grand Victorian buildings rose above her, red brick with wide bay windows. She buttoned her Vivienne Westwood coat – a charity-shop find – and wrapped her scarf around her neck. Her hair was static from where she'd pulled her wool dress on. She smoothed it down and turned left, heading for the bus stop which would take her back to the park.

She blocked out Friday mornings from her usual clients to draw the locals who visited the park's café. Her favourites were the creatures of routine, like the woman who meditated each morning beneath the canopy of an ash tree. She liked drawing the same people over the months and years, recording how they changed and aged. Some would sit for her over tea and cake, others she sketched hurriedly, in a few bare strokes, like the professional dog walkers with their cephalopod leads, or the joggers in psychedelic yoga pants who ran laps past the window.

This was how she escaped the self-conscious way her clients held their bodies, features arranged. She despaired at how they tried to disguise a once broken nose with an awkward tilt of the head, or one over-plucked eyebrow with a hair swoop. She wanted to tell them she loved their lazy eye, their oversized nose. Her first crush had a fine layer of dark fuzz on her upper lip. It was almost imperceptible, like soft arm hair, but once a month the downy line would turn red-raw and stubbly for a few days before growing back a darker colour, the hairs wiry and more pronounced. She adored that moustache.

Her phone was ringing. She stared at the flashing photo of Bettie, her long teeth in a perfect row, the pink of her gums. She swiped the screen and raised it to her ear.

'Are you mad I couldn't make it? I'm sorry. I shouldn't—'

'I'm not even mad. I'm just—'

'Disappointed?'

'Exactly.'

'I'm sorry, I'm sorry. Tell me, how was it? What did he say?'

Mia paused. 'I wish you'd taken the morning off.'

'It's not that easy with school, you know that. Tell me what he said.'

'All on track. Ready for harvesting. I got the last shot.'

Bettie exhaled loudly. 'Oh, Mia. That's wonderful.'

'Do you mean that?'

'Yes, yes. How could you even ask? Look, I know I'm a total arsehole. I have to get back to class. I'll see you at home and we can celebrate? Kombucha or something. Love you.'

Mia hung up. When she and Bettie first met, she searched and searched for some idiosyncrasy – a crooked elbow or a putrid mole on her behind. She found nothing. Bettie was unerringly ordinary. Short, size twelve, black bobbed hair, round dark brown eyes, plain symmetrical face. Her clothes were neat and considered – navy and grey, high-street brands. Her body was solid: firm somehow, even where she was soft. Not even her feet, the easiest of culprits, were offensive. Mia rubbed coconut lotion into them at night, slotting the gaps of her fingers between the gaps of Bettie's toes before slipping one into her mouth.

Telling Bettie made it real. She felt a slight grip of panic. Soon Dr Richards's gossamer gloves would plant embryos in her uterus. Zygote. Eight-cell. Morula. Blastocyst. She tried to picture the fertilized embryos as hydrangeas, their cluster of petals waiting to bloom, round and expansive. If they were lucky, an inner cell mass would become a baby. The trophectoderm would turn into placenta. The fluid-filled cavity would form the yolk sac. Dr Richards would grade her embryos by how well he thought they'd perform. She already mourned the grade ones and twos who only had a twenty per cent chance of implantation. As the eldest of four, she knew all about unfairness.

She turned on to Victoria Park Road. Every time her thighs swished past each other she imagined a pattern of white thumbprints across the inside of her vagina, like a patch of recently touched burnt skin. She couldn't shake the feeling of being prised open, thoughts of Petri dishes, incubators designed to mimic the fallopian tube. All the talk of pH levels reminded her of soap commercials, strips of white paper turning red with acidity. Don't turn red, she pleaded with her soon-to-be-harvested eggs. She adjusted her sticky knickers through her tights.

At the west gate, the usual crayon-green ring of beech trees were winter-spindly, branches the colour of dirty bones, trunks thick and rough. A few burnished leaves were strewn across the ground like litter. The sky had lost its light and turned a blank grey. The wind carried a lone blue balloon until its string tangled with the branches of a tree. It spun, angry in the turbulent air. She much preferred the park in spring. Green was the colour of envy and greed, but it was fresh and innocent too. The colour of growth.

Mona was walking by the lake, its water feature frozen, an arc of ice suspended mid-flight. Mia saw her in the café sometimes, usually with her husband. She'd been to an exhibition about dementia once, seen the slices of freeze-dried brain which got smaller and smaller as they deteriorated with the disease. She'd wondered if the brain decided which moments would hold, or if there was some kind of glue or resin that stuck the important things in place.

The café door was heavy and she pushed hard. Christmas decorations made from cinnamon bark hung from the domed ceiling, stars and bauble shapes twisting in the wind. A net of dangling yellow fairy lights ran in vertical lines along one wall. Inside smelled different. Early morning, the homeless men and women who came in for cups of free tea left behind their scent of dirty wool and dry tobacco. But now she was hit with Sudocrem and sweet milk from the Hot Mums who met there at eleven most days. It was usually Mia's cue to leave. The Hot Mums were cappuccino drinkers, nude lip-gloss wearers, sheathed in Saint Laurent leisurewear, organic cotton skimming all the right places. They talked loudly about time schedules for Monkey Movement classes, Baby Barre workouts, post-partum bodies, how one feeding can burn off the equivalent of a glazed doughnut. As they gesticulated, their breasts bounced like jellies in moulds.

The babies screeched and shrilled, rolling around a mat on the floor like bright marbles, furling and unfurling their fists, moving, exploring, searching for something to put in their mouths. She considered drawing them, but didn't have the focus today to tackle their undefined joints, their lack of knotted ankles and hard elbows. The toddlers used a chair to pull themselves up then fell down. Up, then down. They were the newest generation to be born by the park, would grow up close to good schools, art galleries, acclaimed restaurants, and all that green open space. If Mia fell pregnant, they'd have to leave their too-small, too-expensive flat and retire to the Zone 6 suburbs. They'd end up grateful to be close to a Morrisons. One of them would need to learn to drive.

She queued for coffee. The fairy lights clicked on, then off. On, then off. She stole glances at the Hot Mums and their babies. She recognized one of them as the woman she'd seen viewing Monty's old house. She missed him. Mia had watched Monty for a long time before they first spoke and he'd agreed to sit for her. She liked the tweed suits he wore all year round, even when his broad forehead beaded with sweat. Everything about him was upright, erect, except for his doughy eyelids. He had exquisite hands, which always rested on his knees, poised and polite, like someone interviewing for a job. The skin on the backs of his hands puddled like draped fabric but there was something nimble about the fingers, even the cruel marks where pins had cut the flesh.

One of the babies squealed. She touched her own belly, told herself to relax. To not feel any pressure. It could take months, years. Even then, it might not work. She should prepare herself for that.

The girl behind the counter had clocked her and was already making a decaf soy flat white. They exchanged comments about the cold weather. With a sigh, she ordered sugar-free vegan carrot cake, not the jam dough-nut, and took a seat at her usual table by the window, its varnish grooved by cutlery carelessly scraped across the surface. She wrapped her hands around the china coffee cup and let her palms burn a little. She opened her pad and took a thin stick of vine charcoal from her tin, looking around for a face to draw, one that was not self-conscious. She particularly liked how women picked their nose when they thought no one was watch-ing; relaxed their legs so that they parted invitingly. But, save for the Hot Mums, the café was quiet. An old man reading a Patricia Highsmith in the corner. The girl at the counter swiped through her phone, sucking on her teeth a little.

Mia prodded the carrot cake on the plate in front of her. It had the texture of mushrooms. She took a bite. Without any sugar, the vegetal flavour expanded in her mouth. The café used to serve jacket potatoes with beans and cheese, quiche Lorraine and chicken mayo sandwiches on flat white bloomers. Now it catered to vegans and the health-conscious. Plates were piled high with quinoa and raw carrot batons guarding baba ganoush. The change in appetite had come almost covertly. The russet potatoes switched out for sweet ones; Hovis white sliced for sourdough. Muffins, once yolky yellow, crispy at the edges and studded with chocolate chips, were replaced by banana and bran and a curious mild brown colour to prove it. She longed for sticky-coated teeth. Refined white sugar. But Dr Richards had given her strict instructions. No alcohol, no dairy, no sugar, lots of water, multivitamins, high-quality proteins every few hours, acupuncture once a week, abdominal massage once a month, exercise. Definitely no marijuana. *This is my body*, she wanted to scream. *Mine.*

She shifted in her seat. Crossed and uncrossed her legs. The chair opposite scraped along the floor. She looked up.

'Oh hello,' Mia said, bracing herself to not be recognized. 'How are you? I haven't seen you for a bit.'

Mona frowned. 'Is that a birthmark on your bottom lip?'

She briefly touched her mouth. 'Yes. People try to wipe it off, like I'm a messy eater or something.'

'How unfortunate. It's enormous.'

Mia laughed. 'I've grown to like it.'

'I can't imagine why. But your face is lovely enough to carry it. Lucky to have olive skin.'

Mona relaxed into the wooden chair and shrugged off her coat. The movement released the scent of powdery rose. The café's warm light brought out amber tones in her watery hazel eyes and showed up the sleep lodged in one tear duct. Her lashes were pale and straight, pointing away from thin arched eyebrows and towards a long nose. A wash of pink lipstick enlivened bitten, chapped lips. Her cheeks glistened with a layer of thick moisturizer. Mia longed to draw her.

Mona turned and looked out of the window and Mia followed her gaze. The sun had emerged from behind the clouds. Pigeons were snapping at food scraps on the ground. A small boy and girl were trying to scare one of the birds, shrieking, 'Shoo! Shoo!' in imitations of war cries they must've picked up from TV. The bird flew away and the little girl shouted, 'Come back, come back,' and burst into tears.

'You'll see,' Mona said. 'In a minute the girl will be laughing so hard it'll make you laugh too.' She touched Mia's pad. 'You draw?' she asked.

Mia took a breath and began their routine.

'Yes, I paint with oil, usually. Portraits. But I like to draw with charcoal too. I studied fine art but you have to keep working at it to be any good.'

'How tiresome.'

'It is! I had more energy when I was still a student. I went to every art show I could crash. I could barely afford the paint – we used to shoplift at art shops. But I didn't make great work. I never took things as far as they could go. In the end there was always something else I wanted to do. Go on a date. See a movie. Lie in the sunshine. I couldn't give my work everything. I kept wondering what other life was out there for me.'

Mona frowned. 'Other lives.'

Mia leaned in. 'I was just sketching. Want to see?' She handed her the pad.

Mona flicked through the pages. 'Boring!' she said. And then she stopped. 'Oy gevalt, it's Monty.'

'Yes, we both used to catch the 388 in the mornings up to the Tube.'

'He's an old friend of ours,' Mona was saying. 'Best man at our wedding. Was. Was an old friend. He's passed. I keep. I keep forgetting.'

Mia reached across the table to touch Mona's hand. It was cold and the skin was paper-thin with a bluish tint. She had a sense that it had once been creamy and rich like condensed milk.

'He's at Golders Green Cemetery if you want to have a natter. Wolfie took me. I wanted to tell Monty what's been happening but when I got there I had nothing to say. Nothing at all. I pulled weeds. I did see a woman sitting on a deckchair by a grave, though. A deckchair! Quite the conversation she was having with the headstone.'

Mia nodded then studied the water glass in front of her, its surface marked by the faint imprint of dozens of lipsticked lips, their pinks and reds too earnest to succumb to the dishwasher. Mona released her grip and slipped her fingers beneath the gold bangles that circled Mia's arms. They jingled softly.

'These are beautiful.' Mona stroked her palm then squeezed the fingers one by one with her thumb and middle finger.

'They were a twenty-first birthday present from my mum.'

Mona frowned and they fell into a silence which made Mia realize the Hot Mums had gone. She turned around. Used wet wipes, juice cartons with the life squeezed out of them and a few grapes were squashed into the floor.

'My mother gave me a watch,' Mona said. 'Did I dream it?' Her gaze focused on the window. 'There's the station platform, my mother's shoulders, the watch. We came on the Kindertransport train, Wolfie and I. My mother put me on the train. That was that.'

'I'd no idea you were a Kindertransport kid.'

'Why would you?'

Mia swallowed. She didn't always play her part in this dance very well. 'We learned about Kindertransport in school. I can't even imagine.' She trailed off. She thought of her parents' large stone cottage, white walls and parquet floor. The warm Aga, a little wooden bench by the oven door where her mum read the paper in the mornings. Dachshunds, bracken, and heather. Such safety there, no chance of anything unusual happening, so she'd left as soon as she could. Now she loved returning home, loved its familiarity and comfort. She was looking forward to Christmas, big meals, an open fire, long walks. She wondered if Mona's mum had feared that her daughter might never come home, and what did that mean, the idea of returning, if you and the place and the people you once knew were about to change forever?

'The watch had a lovely face. So lovely. I couldn't read Roman numerals.' Mona's face creased into confusion.

She guessed Mona hadn't had much help dealing with childhood trauma in her life. Mia had been in therapy before, so when Dr Richards had advised them to start counselling she'd found it easier than Bettie. They'd chosen a female counsellor in a smart Barbican practice and lasted one session. The room was cream, a single rubber plant in the corner. Mia found the blank walls empowering. They'd both blurted out their concerns. So many things that couldn't be taken back, like: *You haven't even come out at work. How can I be sure I'll love it? What if you don't get your figure back? I'm afraid you'll turn into your mother.*

'Let me get you some tea,' Mia said. 'Something to eat?'

'No, no. I'm fine. Fine.' Mona swept her finger along Mia's plate and lifted the crumbs to her mouth. 'Terrible cake,' she said, wrinkling her nose.

Mia laughed. The café was filling up with early lunchers. They brought in the cold as they trooped through the door and crowded the counter, ordering with loud fast voices, accents of all kinds.

'If you're feeling up to it, I've always wanted to draw you.'

'Go ahead. It's nice to be sitting.'

'Let me get you tea and some cake first, I insist. Or a sandwich? It's getting to be that time.'

'Feh! Everyone is always trying to feed me. I'm not a child.'

'Nothing? You're sure?'

'Nothing.' Mona waved dismissively. She re-tucked her grey cashmere roll-neck into dogtooth slacks. They sat high on her narrow waist and she plucked at the waistband distractedly. Four thick gold art deco rings hung loosely from her slender fingers. A small ruby caught the light.

'OK. So don't think about your body. Relax for me. Whenever you want to stop, just say.'

Mia turned to a fresh page in her sketchbook, palmed her hand across the texture of its calico surface. She pulled a thicker stick of charcoal from her tin. The noise of the café settled to a low hum as customers devoured their food.

Usually the first outline came to her in broad confident strokes but it was different with Mona. Although her head was still, her expression kept moving, memories or moments lapping like waves at the edges of her features. Mia started with her forehead, its thin trail of lines that began at one eye and ended at the other. Two dark brown moles on her chin. Criss-crossing swollen veins which marked her neck.

'I'm not a child,' Mona said quietly. 'I *have* a child.'

Mona had never mentioned a child before.

'A little girl,' she said, smiling. 'Ester.' Something in her face shifted. Mona looked down at her stomach. 'I know. I know I had a daughter. She died young. We don't speak about it. Whooping cough.'

'I'm so sorry,' Mia managed. She wondered – when the memory resurfaces, does it cut like new?

Mona's face changed abruptly so that it became impossibly blank, like a slammed door. 'I'd. I'd almost forgotten. There seems to be so much to forget. I'm a leaky bucket.' She paused and leaned in closer. 'I know they tell Wolfie to put me in a home,' she whispered. 'I'm not stupid. He knows I'm fine. I just forget things. He looks after me.'

Mia held her breath and looked back at her pad. She didn't know what to say so she smudged the edges of

Mona's cheekbones, making shadows. She put the charcoal down.

'Do you have children?' Mona asked.

'Actually, we're trying now with IVF.'

Mona laughed. 'You making up words?'

Mia shook her head. 'We need extra help to conceive from a doctor. It's a whole process.' She turned to the window. People passed by, pulling their coats closer as the cold scissored through gaps in fake fur, pillowy black parkas. The curve of their backs interested her, the way they steadied themselves against the wind. But generally people were the least like themselves in winter: there was too much opportunity for disguise, to be buttoned up to the neck, to hide beneath a low-slung hat.

Mona flapped at a fruit fly. 'Heavens,' she said. 'Is your husband excited to be a father?'

'Well my partner Bettie is pretty ambivalent about the whole thing, if I'm honest.' She swallowed. It was not something she'd admitted to anyone before.

'There you are then. You need a thingy to make babies! No wonder you can't get pregnant! Get yourself a nice husband like my Wolfie.'

She laughed, and picked up the charcoal and built in the fine waves of Mona's hair. It was beautiful, set in a rippling forties style, a few strands straying from the fold. 'He's a nice man, your Wolfie. I used to see him in the deli.'

'Babies come from love, my dear, not a stork. You can't do it alone.' Mona tilted her head, appraising Mia.

'It's all a bit complicated,' Mia said quietly. She bent her head closer to the page then pulled back to look at it from further away. It was missing something but she couldn't figure out what. It irked her. 'Maybe we should stop here for today,' she said. 'Let me walk you home.'

'Oh no, please finish the drawing. This is nice.'

Mia hesitated. 'I'll get you some tea first. I insist.' She rose from the chair too quickly and a stabbing pain shot between her legs. She walked to the queue with a wider gait than normal, and ordered another decaf coffee and an English breakfast tea. As she waited, she stared out at the lake. A swan's feathers ruffled in the wind, and smaller ducks struggled across its bumpy surface. The fountain in the middle had thawed in the brief noon sun and now water shot out in a wide spray, blowing sideways like a curtain by an open window.

Placing the teapot in front of Mona, she poured. The brown liquid streamed into the cup.

'Say when for milk.'

Mona took the tea and dipped her head close to its steam. The steam.

Mia took the charcoal and drew the outline of a steam train emerging from Mona's right ear and curling around the top of the page. She gave it a sweeping curve, oversized wheels, and used her fingers to soften the spokes.

She imagined Mona as a child in the window, her silhouette in profile, facing forwards, abandoned in one sense, set free in another. She wanted to know: Who else was left behind? Did Mona risk looking back at her mother until she was rendered a black dot, or stare out into the landscape, and if she did, what did she see? Trees and rivers rushing by her? The familiar turning into the unfamiliar, or was it all foreign to her, the platform, the train tracks, the city and then the green?

She decided against adding tracks, just a few single lines beneath the train as if it were picking up speed and leaving the page, passengers appearing in rapid frames, rushing off into a future violently flung in front of them.

Mia wanted to know which of her own features sitting in her embryos were about to come to life. The shape of her eyes? Her high forehead? Would her mother's psoriasis be passed down? The predisposition for breast cancer from her grandmother? What would it be like, never to see Bettie in their child's face?

Mona leaned across the table, stroked Mia's cheek, and then turned up her palms. 'Look,' she said. 'You're crying.' Mona handed her a coarse brown serviette.

Mia touched her face. 'I think, I think I might be a bit overwhelmed. Hormones.'

'My child,' Mona said. 'Dear sweet girl. It can't be that bad.' Mona squeezed her hands. 'Come, what do I look like?'

Mia turned the sketchbook. Mona looked bemused. She cocked her head to the side. 'That's not me. I'm not *so* old. It's my mother! You've drawn my mother.'

Mia looked again at the drawing. It wasn't great – Mona's face was much bolder than in reality – but it was a start. 'This deserves colour,' she said. 'It shouldn't be grey. I'm going to paint it. Azure and turquoise, seascape colours, sky colours – I've never really used those before. Something to show that it's taking flight. Greens too, for spring.'

It would mark a departure from her usual style. She would work and rework it until she got it right. She stood and linked her arm with Mona's. 'Let's get you home,' she said.

'I don't want to leave my home,' Mona said. 'Don't let them do that to me.'

She laid her head on Mia's shoulder as they walked. 'Sweet girl,' she murmured.

Outside, the wind had passed. The air was still. Mia looked up. Birds flew in formation towards the café roof. The sky glowed white above their heads.

January

Broken Biscuits

The silence of the deli felt so accusatory that Luca picked up his phone again, despite promising himself to stop scrolling. Shrieks and laughter burst into the room. It felt as if his mates back home were videoing themselves having a good time just to emphasize the banality of pound coins slipping through his fingers as he did the evening cash-up. Just to remind him how everyone had now reached the conventional marrying age and he'd missed yet another wedding because he couldn't afford the time off. He placed the phone face down on the counter. Fifteen minutes until closing time, and then it was band practice and the night was his.

Luca's hand hovered over the phone again, but he reached into the till instead, and counted the fifty-pence coins. He recorded the final amount on Wolfie's archaic cashing-up sheet, and put it into the finance box on top of the previous day's entry. The marble counter top received a final spritz of sanitizer before it was wiped away with a J Cloth and then he picked up the phone again. He scrolled a little more, put in his earphones, selected a Sun Ra playlist, and slipped into the well-worn fantasy of his other life as a world-class jazz musician.

This reverie was broken by Joe, who honked the horn on his Vespa with the same gusto he used to hit his drum kit. Joe's childlike delight in creating loud sounds reminded Luca of when his kids first discovered pots and pans. He waved at his friend through the window, and then flicked off the lights. Locking the door behind him, he used his whole body weight to pull down the metal shutters, overcoming their shuddering resistance.

It was already dark outside, and Luca stopped to button up his overcoat and wind a wool scarf around his neck.

Joe held out a black helmet. 'Happy Wednesday, mate.'

'Happy Wednesday,' he replied, clapping Joe lightly on the back. He lifted the helmet over his head but stopped to frown at the crude space on the rear of Joe's bike where his recently stolen number plates should be. 'We'll get pulled over,' he said.

Joe grinned. 'Relax.' The wind whipped his tie from the constraints of his bomber jacket and Joe tucked it back in. He patted the leather seat behind him. 'Hop on. We'll be late. Don't want Col having kittens.'

The helmet's foam lining crushed Luca's curls and he fiddled with the chinstrap. Joe's shiny black brogue pushed down on the kick-starter and the engine coughed into life. 'Remind me later to play you this new Israeli-American jazz drummer,' Joe shouted over his shoulder. 'Unreal. Guy has mad skills.'

Joe weaved the scooter in and out of cars and buses as they fought their way up to Cambridge Heath Road. At the lights, Luca watched two of Joe's fingers break free from their grip on the handlebar, tap-tapping a frenetic rhythm on the rubber surface. They took off through Bethnal Green towards Bishopsgate, the Gherkin, and then the city hurtled by until Luca's eyes watered. He closed them for a moment, feeling the wind blast the day from his skin, the scream of the engine drowning out the sounds of the metropolis.

The chrome body of the bike slanted as Joe took the corners too fast, and Luca tightened his grip around his friend's slim waist. They dipped and curved through the streets, speeding past the droves of pedestrians as they walked with heads lowered against the wind. Colourful rain jackets and baseball caps marked the tourists out among the dark overcoats and tan trenches of workers rushing from their glass offices.

Soon they were passing some of the city's most impressive buildings, the ones he'd been in awe of when he first arrived – St Paul's, Somerset House, the Brutalist cubes of the Hayward Gallery visible now across the Thames. They reached Waterloo bridge, and the diamond structures that blocked either side of the pavement forced him to wonder – could they really stop a truck if it was going full speed? How many people were stabbed in that terrorist attack?

An aeroplane emerged from the clouds. Seagulls flew low over the water, circling, and, beyond the dark and the fog, the moon was only a faint suggestion.

The Broken Biscuits rehearsed in a basement studio beneath Waterloo station. It was built in the seventies, when punk bands shouted and smashed their way through practice, turning the walls a slurry grey with cigarette smoke. Joe financed their band rehearsals with whatever it was he did in Canary Wharf, and had struck a deal with the building manager – a one-time roadie for the Sex Pistols, and Joe's ex-heroin-dealer.

Joe and Luca arrived ahead of the twins Col and Henrique. Joe disappeared to the toilet, and Luca settled at the piano, texting Elena to remind her that there was a jar of yesterday's pesto to drizzle over the lasagne he'd left in the fridge. He let his fingers lightly pass over the keys, and then sang the beginning of a ditty he'd composed for Lydia. 'There are five pandas on the moon/ who'd like to meet you and sing you a tune.'

'Christ, what's that? Bit camp, isn't it?'

Luca looked up and saw an unlit spliff between Joe's lips. He groaned. 'Thought you were quitting?'

'I do what I want on band night.' Joe flicked the top of a pink Hello Kitty lighter a girl had likely left on his bedside table, and released a rotting herbal stench into the already musty air.

Luca raised a brow. 'You do what you want every night.'

Joe exhaled. 'True.' He examined the tip of his joint. 'You know, I've *earned* this. Tomorrow, it's eight years since I stopped using H. And since NA kicked me out for still smoking weed—'

'—and drinking,' Luca interrupted.

'—*and* drinking, I'm celebrating my own way.' Joe inhaled again deeply, breathed out. 'That's better.'

'My friend, if nothing else, you would play better if you stayed sober.'

'Narc.' Joe sighed. 'Honestly, I love that girl, but since Lyddie was born you've outdone yourself on the boring scale.'

Luca did not respond. Had he been boring for nine years? He knew his friend had an acid tongue, but it was usually aimed at other people. Joe was like a brother, his first friend in London. He didn't expect to take the same kind of ribbing from him as Angelo, his actual brother, doled out.

'How was the deli today?' Joe asked.

Luca shrugged and moved from the piano to join Joe on the sagging sofa that faced the small stage. 'Wolfie was fussing about the cream-cheese supplier again. It was quiet. Lunch rush, then –' he swept a hand through the air '– nothing. Meant I had time to think more about Elena's song, though.'

Joe straightened. 'What's that?'

'You know the one, "Adelaide".' He paused. 'Think I've fixed the looping sax refrain – that's how she unravels her bun when she comes home from work.' He unbuttoned his collar and scratched his head.

'You've a hole in the armpit,' Joe said, gesturing at Luca's shirt. He waved a flame again across the tip of his smouldering joint. 'I didn't know that song was about her.' Joe smiled. 'You're so soft,' he said, digging Luca in the ribs.

Joe stood and walked to the drum kit in the centre of the room. The guitar and bass cabs were either side, with a row of microphones and the piano next to a small PA system. He perched on his stool, his blue eyes reddening. 'How're things?'

'Same same. No change with the long shifts, then studying at night when the kids are in bed. It's a lot.'

'I think the less time Elena spends at home, the more you revere her.'

Before Luca could protest, the door swung open and Henrique and Col walked in. They both had long brown hair and thickly-lashed doe eyes, and wore utilitarian-style button-up shirts.

'Lads,' Henrique said, nodding at Joe and Luca.

Col dug into the plastic bag hanging from his wrist. 'Grub's up,' he said, handing them each a kofta. 'It's lamb.'

Luca smiled, grateful for one day in the week when the role of feeder did not fall to him. He took a warm wrap, ripped off the top of the greaseproof paper, set aside the pickled yellow chilli, and chomped down on the salty meat. Creamy garlic sauce oozed from the sides.

From the pocket of his shirt jacket, Henrique pulled a mini bottle of Atomic Hot Sauce and upended it on to his kebab.

Luca swallowed. 'Criminal,' he said, and shook his head.

Henrique took an enormous mouthful, chewed half of it and replied, 'Makes everything taste good.'

Joe ate silently, then leaned over and snatched Luca's chilli from the table.

'Hey!' Luca said.

'It's the best bit and you just left it there.' Joe's pointing finger drummed the side of the table with a light but insistent thud-thud. 'More fool you.'

'I was saving it!'

'Let's start,' Henrique interrupted. 'I've got two hours without the kids and I wouldn't mind a couple of pints after practice before I go home and listen to the missus tell me all my shortcomings.'

Col pulled a sweet from his shirt pocket, popped it in his mouth and rubbed the wrapper between his thumb and middle finger to make a synthetic swish-swish sound, before he snapped open the buckles of his saxophone case, spurring everyone else into action.

'OK, let's start with "Transistor",' Joe said.

Luca wiped his mouth with the back of his hand and settled himself on the gnarled stool so that his body was level with the upright piano. He loved that piano. Its cabinet was black and glossy, eighty-five per cent wood, polyester resin. It was no Steinway, but it was elegant, the raw materials fine and tenderly chosen not just for aesthetics but for sound. And what a sound! He considered the impact that the first note was about to make, a mid F sharp, as he sat straight and poised, fingers hovering over the keys. The mechanics of the instrument had always fascinated him. Soon those keys would strike the wooden hammers hidden inside, their heads wrapped in soft felt, each one sounding their designated note. A split second later the damper would stop the vibrations and cease the sound, making way for the next note like a gentleman opening the door for a lady.

Joe counted them in.

And then there it was – the clear F sharp bursting from the cast-iron plate over the soundboard, which shook and groaned and spluttered out the amplified vibrations of the strings, giving Joe his cue to stamp the bass drum – pale gold with a hint of glitter – which released a succession of percussive pulses that Luca followed with his keys. The gleaming brass of Col's saxophone caught the overhead lights as he raised it to his lips. One beat, two beat, then Henrique joined in, his head bent over the double bass as if in prayer, hair brushing the fingerboard. The flamed maple and spruce of his bass had been finished with an amber stain, highlighting the grains of the wood like markings on a tiger hide. He plucked the strings and the faint lines of his forehead moved with the frequency of a heart monitor, up and down, up and down.

But as practice continued, Luca winced as Col stumbled over the notes, never quite getting it together. Song after song missed the mark. Henrique was slow, Joe skipped a beat – he always skipped a beat, rushing or dragging through the music depending on how much he'd smoked. Luca tried to concentrate on his own instrument, get the best from what he was working with, but his spirits were sinking.

They moved into 'Cedar Dreams'.

'Stop, stop,' Joe cried. 'Nothing sounds right, guys. Let's start from the top.'

'Why don't we try "Adelaide"? I want to record it,' Luca said, getting out his phone. 'Get a feel for what's missing.' Joe shrugged and Henrique nodded.

Luca handed Col a sheet of music. 'I've been working on that opening phrase.'

Joe counted them in and then Col opened the song. Slow, smoky notes eased out of the sax. Luca's feet lifted up and then down, left and then right. In his head, he sang the lyrics he'd written about Elena. He knew they were full of clichés and barely concealed anxiety. The song was less of a romantic gesture and more of a tragic opera, really. But as they continued to play, he felt the music transforming into the kind of electric elixir he usually only experienced when he listened to Charlie Parker or George Duke. It was working. It sounded – right. Maybe it was even their best one yet.

He opened his eyes and took in the room. Everyone was smiling in private, concentrated ways, preoccupied with the sound, with keeping on top of each second passing. The music was vibrating in their bones, he was sure of it. Outside, the black sky would be sagging over the city, the air paper-cut sharp, but in here they were sweating in unison, warm and glowing.

The band played the last note and stopped, each member grinning at the other in surprise until they burst into laughter.

'Guys, that was great,' Henrique said.

'Synchronicity,' Luca agreed. 'I didn't know we could be that good.'

Col nodded solemnly. 'It felt, I dunno, truthful. If we

work a bit more on the middle eight, make it flow like the rest of the song, it'd be perfect.'

Joe opened a Tupperware box and offered up a pile of hash brownies. Luca took the largest piece, though he hadn't got high in years.

'Ah, there he is,' Joe said. 'You know what, I think we could really be *going* places. Like, there's something here, man.'

Luca grinned, and ran his tongue over the chocolate that coated his front teeth.

'But after all that embarrassment at Ronnie Scott's...' Henrique trailed off.

'It's different now,' Joe said. 'We've worked hard. Gotten better. It's time to book gigs.' He produced a six-pack of beers and cracked the ring. 'Put the latest stuff up on SoundCloud.'

Luca tuned out of the chat, trying to hold on to the feeling of getting it right, to determine how it happened so they could achieve it again. But as the weed hit his bloodstream, he began to feel loose-boned, and the specifics of the evening eluded him, becoming instead an abstract – a beautiful, unpredictable thing, like the patterns of freckles on Elena's skin.

Luca's body thrilled with a pulsing light. The dark was spliced with the tangerine glow of street lamps. It made him ache for something sour – a grapefruit would be nice. He floated up from his body and watched himself stumble along the Thames Path to the bus stop. He was conspicuously happy.

As he walked, he admired the railway tracks above him, thin interlocking steel lines diverging and converging – a skeleton map which made little sense to anyone but the train driver. And then there was the metallic clang of a train in the distance; a flash of brightly lit carriages, passengers crushed together, all heading somewhere. Luca thought about home. By now Lydia would be tucked beneath her panda sheets, the dog at her feet; maybe Freddy would be on the roof, swaddled in a blanket on the beanbag. Elena would be at the kitchen table, studying for her exams.

At the bus stop, Luca watched two teenage girls as they leaned against the red plastic bench, sharing a set of earphones. One girl had unnaturally dark eyebrows, thickened with pencil; the other small eyes sharpened with globs of mascara. They were both uncomfortably thin, long twiggy legs wrapped in denim so tight it could be cling film. He prayed for Lydia to stay nine years old.

At this time of night, the 388 was demoted to a single-decker and it ambled down the road as if embarrassed. He tapped his bankcard and smiled at the driver who only stared straight ahead. There were three people on the bus already, two on their phones and a third with a paperback, the front cover folded over. Luca sank into the seat behind the reading woman and put in his earbuds, turning his phone volume all the way up to listen to the new recording. He stared out of the window, transfixed by the lurid quality of the Thames rendered brown by the dark.

Luca felt eyes on him. He turned, music still blaring.

'Excuse me,' mouthed the reader. 'What's that you're listening to?'

He slipped the buds from his ears, noticed a fleck of yellow wax and flicked it off.

The woman was younger than him, early twenties maybe, with a serious but open face. She wore a beanie, pale hair spilling out from beneath it on to her shoulders.

'Oh I'm sorry, it's too loud,' he said.

The song continued to play, Joe's cymbals the only discernible sound.

'No no, it's nice. Can I listen?'

He smiled and shrugged. 'Of course, if you want. It's my band, the Broken Biscuits.' He swiped back to the beginning of the track and handed her the phone.

She took off her hat, and Luca watched as her eyes widened and the apples of her cheeks became more pronounced. Her expression was delicate and lively, like a small child.

'It's so great,' she mouthed.

'You think?'

'Yeah.' She removed the earbuds. 'When's your next gig? I'd love to come watch.'

'We just goof around at practice, really, trying to get good.'

'You should put something online,' she said, ringing the bell. 'This is me.'

Luca walked past the deli, its grey shutters silver in the moonlight. The streets around the park were silent, cars parked bumper to bumper. He found himself longing for a cigarette, though he hadn't had one since Elena first fell pregnant. He noticed a BMW in front of Monty's house, its dark muscular body incongruous beside the Victorian facade. Had the house already been bought? Poor Monty, healthy as anything and then bam – heart attack and it was all over.

Approaching his end of the street, the darkness was punctuated with the light from four windows, shadows of movement playing across the panes of glass. He caught the indistinct profile of the old woman who lived opposite before she tugged at the netting and disappeared. Through Mona and Wolfie's living-room window, he saw the glare of the TV and he wondered which one of them couldn't sleep. Monty's death had unnerved Wolfie, the suddenness of it all, and he'd been more irritable than usual.

There was the drone of a car in the distance, and then

the road was silent again save for the high-pitched thrum from the electricity cables, and the rustle of overfed squirrels, their plump bodies scrabbling through bushes at the edge of the park. It was those kinds of noises that made him miss the family farm. As a kid, he'd always risen early, long before Angelo, and watched the landscape wake up through his bedroom window. In summer, the sunrise would cross their neat garden, the fields beyond, and bathe the scorched bricks of the outhouses. And then, when the livestock stirred, their crunching and snuffling combined with the throbbing hum of insects and the operatic rumble of the tractor. In winter, the snow would disfigure his view, warp the hills into something new, as if the house had been transplanted elsewhere during the night. But his parents' voices were always the same as they went about breakfast. Fetta biscottata, or ciambellone. Caffè latte warming on the stove to be sipped from the same blue bowl.

And through the window he'd watch Marine when she accompanied her father on his veterinary visits. Once he had seen her help deliver a calf in distress. He was gripped by the silent, private process she shared with her father as they manoeuvred around the heifer in the spooling floodlight, could not deny a vague erotic charge as her arm disappeared into the beast. It was Marine he had hoped to see the night he'd gone to the local bar and met Elena for the first time.

He should never have allowed his brother to sell the farm. But when their parents died, Angelo took charge. He flew back from London, put the farm on the market, and organized a lavish and speedy wedding before anyone could notice Elena's bump. He brought the teenage couple back with him and Luca's share of the inheritance was spent on a down payment for a small flat on the west corner of Victoria Park.

The park was what had saved him when they moved to London, from his grief, from the shock of its greyness, from the damp. At least here he could see the seasons changing, have a place to walk the dog. Back then, his English was terrible. He despised its strange syntax and grammatical rules, the unnatural ways it forced his tongue to curve. In Veneto, he'd been a commis chef in a popular restaurant. But he spent his first year in London pulling double shifts as a kitchen porter in a Mayfair hotel. 'It's only temporary,' Elena would say. 'Better things are coming.' The precious hours in-between work were taken up with English classes, where he tried to unlock his speech, and putting into practice what he'd learned there at home while cooking. 'I'm going to slice you now,' he'd murmur to the carrots, careful to use the contraction. 'Chop chop.' The one indulgence in his new life was jazz, and he spent a few pounds each Sunday buying records from Rafello's stall on Brick Lane which he'd play on a seventies Sony PS-4750 turntable.

But living around the park was also a reminder of what others had. Net worth was determined by whether there were stone steps leading up to your house, or a front drive with a Toyota Yaris or an Audi – both, sometimes – parked there, set back from the road. Luca's windows were street-level and the high heels which hit the pavement outside echoed as if strangers were walking through your living room. Snippets of zealous phone calls punctuated family mealtimes with their abrupt one-sidedness.

He walked the last few yards slowly now, caught in the somnolence of sobering up, holding his phone in his palm and running his fingers over the smooth black screen so that every so often it woke up and flashed a picture of Freddy and Lydia laughing as they both tried to climb on to Elena's lap. He had taken the photo five or six years ago on a beach in Sicily. Their last family holiday.

There was a light on in the kitchen. He pushed open the back door and poured his body through with the same exaggerated care he'd seen Freddy take trying to disguise a night of teenage drinking. The warmth and sudden tangy smell of pesto hit him and he looked at the kitchen through his new, stoned, perspective. Keith Jarrett had provided the soundtrack when he'd stripped the walls of their browning paper all those years ago, Freddy strapped to his back, lulled to sleep by the rhythm and flair of the bass. He built the units himself, found the table and chairs at the second-hand furniture dealer under the railway arches. He'd always taken joy in their flat, proud of what he'd provided for his family, but now he saw it was unremarkable. A low ceiling, cramped, full of worn furniture. He knew Elena hadn't wanted to stay here so long – she'd thought of it as a place for a few years, not nearly two decades. He looked up and realized he'd never liked the dark green cabinet which she'd painted on a whim.

And there she was at the table just as he'd imagined, headphones on, bent over a textbook, her long honey-coloured hair twisted into a practical knot at the nape of her neck, exposing the freckles that began at the top of her spine and tracked their way down to her coccyx. Her features were pursed together in concentration – generally speaking, her expression hadn't changed for years. He bumped into the side of the oven and swore.

Her head snapped up. 'Jesus, Luca!' she said. 'You scared me!' She paused, arranging a deeper frown. 'What's wrong with your face?'

'I ate one of Joe's hash brownies,' he said. 'Didn't think it'd be so strong.' He studied the old wood planks of the floor. 'I feel great, though. Mellow.'

'I thought Joe had quit getting high.' She sighed. 'There's some leftover lasagne in the fridge if you want.'

Luca reached for the fruit bowl, pulling out a clementine and holding it to the light to observe its perfect sphere.

'How was your day? We played the best we've ever played tonight. I made a recording of the new song. I'll put it on. This one you might actually like.'

She looked at him with one of her deliberate, bold expressions, leaning back to rest her head against the chair. She pulled out the biro which held her bun in place, and shook her hair free, combing through the strands with her fingers.

He longed to lay his head on her lap. 'You look like a sunflower.'

She arched her eyebrows.

'Seriously.' He plugged his phone into the stereo. 'I mean, everyone was riding the same wave tonight, Elena.' He fiddled with the levels, adjusting the bass. 'Listen.'

The phone recording was surprisingly clear as it ran through the speakers.

'Joe sounds incredible, doesn't he?' He closed his eyes.

Before Luca could turn his attention back to the room, Elena left her books on the table and headed to the bathroom. She closed the door, pulling hard on the rusty metal bolt. Her navy trousers fell to the floor, then her white shirt. She peered into the mirror above the sink and ran her hands across her smooth tanned body, trailing fingertips over the fine white web of stretch marks on her thighs, hips and breasts, before squeezing her eyes tightly shut. She breathed in and out, then opened her eyes again and examined the creases in her forehead. She leaned closer to the mirror, watched her breath mist and then unmist a small circle on the glass. The bath wasn't even half full before she slipped into the warm water and took the showerhead from its rest, aimed it between her legs and lay back, propping her neck on the edge on the tub. In the reflection of the tiles, she imagined she could see the pupils of her eyes widen, pushing against the blue irises. Her breathing quickened. Her chest rose and fell.

So when the song ended, Luca turned and faced an empty room. The kitchen appeared smaller somehow and his lips tingled the same way they did after he ate a disappointing meal – a feeling akin to regret, but with a physical ache to it, a longing for something more substantial. The weed released its prickly side. He began to sink into cloudy despair. He brushed his hand against the polished wood of the counter top. It was reassuringly firm against his damp palm. He stared at the table. The space where Elena had sat seemed more solid, more concrete than when she'd actually been there. He picked up his phone and watched the video of his friends' wedding again. The shrieks and laughter were intrusively loud. He pressed the OFF button on the stereo and in the silence heard the groan of pipes and water rushing into the bathtub.

February

Pale Yellow

Elena was perched on the edge of the toilet, one foot on the bathtub, painting her toenails a colour named Sand Tropez. The little glass bottle was a present from Joe – a gift more for the giver than the receiver. She hadn't painted her nails in years. Joe was in the bath eating a grilled cheese sandwich – his usual room-service order. The plate was balanced on his chest, on top of the meagre hairs he told her had both started and stopped growing at seventeen.

'I'm still kinda hung up about it,' he said, mouth full of half-chewed food. The cheese was the same colour as his teeth. 'Is it more manly to be hairy?'

'No,' she lied. 'My biggest hang-up are these bunions. Can't get rid of them.' She waggled her left foot and he hooked her big toe between his fingers, bringing it to his mouth and kissing the two red bumps.

She squirmed out of his grasp.

He reached for the Ruinart on the floor and tipped it back. She accepted the dregs of the bottle from his outstretched hand, though they'd both had enough. It was four p.m. The bubbles burst in her throat. They tasted of brioche and vanilla, the sweet pastries Luca and the kids favoured in the mornings.

Joe was about to turn thirty-eight. To celebrate, they were at one of London's finest hotels, in a junior suite. He told her he'd chosen it for its take-it-all-in balcony – so the website gushed – with views over Knightsbridge. But to Elena, all expensive hotels were the same. Marble colonnades, intricate stitching on starched uniforms, an abundance of heavy velvet curtains, pleated and finished with gold brocade. All she took in from the balcony was the excessive shopping happening below them, how Uber had yet to conquer the black-cab business in central London. The women who climbed in and out of those bug-shaped cars had glossy hair and shining skin. They moved like gazelles on their thin heels, long bodies sheathed in silk and fur, or else they wore flowing hijabs and had ruby lips. She couldn't fathom having the time to look that polished.

The room was overheated and stuffy, decorated in shades of coffee and cream – a cappuccino nightmare that had cost Joe a packet. She'd been trying not to dwell on the king-size bed big enough to fit her whole family, and, since her period was due, the swathes of pale linen around her.

'Wanna bite before it's gone?' he asked, waving the crust of his sandwich.

'Toast was plenty.'

He shook his head. 'Never met anyone who likes toast as much as you.' He licked crumbs from his fingers, and then dunked his head under the foamy water. It smelled of violets and the lavender suds turned his skin ghostly grey.

'Toast is only a vehicle for butter,' she said when he emerged. 'It's the butter, not the bread. Haven't I told you about my last project at art school?'

'Nope.' He flipped the lid of the miniature shampoo bottle and tipped its contents into his hands, working up lather. 'Spill.'

She lifted her other foot on to the edge of the bathtub and continued painting her toenails. 'My thing was photographing foods that taste like their colour. Cabbage, paprika, you get the gist. I thought it was so original, that's the thing about your first-year art school – you think everything's *new*. Anyway, nothing tastes more like its colour than butter. I'd stack dozens of fridge-cold pats on the studio floor, surround them with heaters then photograph them softening and melting until they became a great pool of pale yellow.'

He laughed. 'Course you did. I always fall for artists. Thought I'd broken it with you being a nurse, but no. I'm doomed to love a creative soul.'

She blinked twice at the word *love*.

'What were you like at art school?' he asked. 'You must've been with Luca by then?'

'I was eager, ambitious. Very naive. But I was only there ten months before I got pregnant.'

Joe dunked his head under again and pushed the dripping hair from his eyes. He'd let it grow over the last few months and it curled around his earlobes now, making him more impish and boy-like. It trailed along her skin when he kissed her body.

'Was it there you discovered your love of butter?'

'It's just such a sensual thing.'

'If you had to choose: me or butter?'

'Butter.'

'I'm a wonderful lay, and you know it,' he said, raising his hips out of the water and flopping his penis from side to side. Even limp it was unreasonably long.

'Sensual isn't the same thing as sexual. Don't be immature.'

'You love it. Get in the tub.'

She shook her head. 'Toenails are wet.'

He stood, scooped her into his arms from behind and then set her down between his legs, banging her foot against the tap. In water, their bodies looked like shadows beneath the bubbles. She felt weightless and desultory, paused in the middle of a dream.

'So lovely,' he murmured, pulling her clip so her hair

travelled down her back. 'Perfect shade of honey. Or wheat. Nature's good stuff.' He grasped her hip, palmed her stomach, played with her navel. She liked the way he manhandled her, the momentary illusion that she was his. He tipped her head, bit her bottom lip, and then pushed his tongue into her mouth. She sucked on it gently. It was thick and flat, like hers. He drew back and asked, 'Are you sick of me yet?'

Two days was the longest time they'd ever spent alone. She slid her hands under the foam and cupped his bony behind, overcome with gratitude at how aroused she was, for the way her body had been returned to her. And though she knew they were in the middle of some kind of catastrophe, it felt as warm as the bathwater – the kind of comfort which alerted you to how cold you were before you got in. It made the idea of getting out again impossible.

Later, Joe told her he skimmed through the first and last page of a book as a way to decide whether it was worth reading.

'That ruins the whole experience,' she said.

'When was the last time you read fiction? No, don't answer that – it's too depressing. Just trust me, it's sensible. Who wants to waste time reading something shit? You can learn everything you need to know about a book by the first and last pages.'

'By that logic, *Moby-Dick* is about a guy named Ishmael who gets depressed sometimes and goes sailing.'

'OK, nice Melville reference. But think about it. All those firsts and lasts that end up being defining moments. First wank, first cheeseburger, first fuck,' he said, counting them off on his fingers. 'Last words.' He scratched his wrist. 'Last time I had a fix.'

She sat up, propping her head on three plump cushions. He smiled at her, fiddling with the small silver hoop in his right ear. What were her important firsts? The first time she developed a photograph, the image gradually appearing through the chemicals, the dunk into the stop bath, the satisfying drip as she pegged it up. Giving birth, the blur of it, then the sweetness of the top of Freddy's head. The first time a patient died on her watch. The first time she cheated on Luca. Moments that existed before she could finesse her thinking and feeling, before she'd made sense of a sensation, before it became a story she told herself. What had led to each of those moments was a mystery, though nothing was as mysterious as her own desire.

She tried to remember the first time she came but the specifics were murky. Growing up, sex was a private performance between her childhood self and the adult she was going to become. She'd first been aroused from the age of eight or nine years old, when she'd rubbed up against her oversized teddy bear at night, face buried in his matted fur. At the time, she didn't have a name for what she was doing but she also couldn't recall any surprise at the sensation. Feeling good was there for the taking. So she took. By the age of ten or eleven, she'd begun to imagine having a grown-up body with breasts and pubic hair, being tall and beautiful – the things she thought were inevitable with adulthood. She never imagined being desired, or having anyone actually beneath her. She didn't think about another person's breath, or scent, or about what their pleasure might look like. She was alone with her need, locked in her body, rubbing and rubbing her poor red vagina until something would burst open and she'd stop.

It was a sweaty, comforting routine which increased in frequency and urgency over time. Everything stayed between her and the stuffed toy. His name was Samuel. Her first and last selfless lover.

Joe was looking at her expectantly. But she was too warm, too alive, too far away from her life to want to share it. Instead, she leaned across the bed and kissed his earlobe. 'Let me pay some attention to those,' she said.

Joe tied a knot in the condom before rolling out of bed to fling it in the bathroom bin. The sheets had puddled on the floor and the undersides of her breasts were sticky with sweat. She was hungry again.

'Tell me about the first girl you kissed,' she said.

The sound of his thunderous peeing erupted through the open door. 'I don't remember her name,' he called out.

'No?'

The toilet flushed and he slid back into bed. He hadn't washed his hands. He lifted his arm and she nestled into the nook of his chest. He smelled pleasantly musty.

'It was at a holiday camp with my best mate's family. A Butlin's maybe? Some arse-end of nowhere. God, I wonder what Jack's up to now. Anyway, I was blotto on Smirnoff Ice – we used a straw to get the air in so you could down it in one go – and we played Spin the Bottle with some girls. I had my first kiss that way. Couldn't tell you who it was.'

'How old were you?'

'Eleven? Twelve maybe?'

'Young to be drunk!'

'Yeah, maybe. You? You owe me a story.'

'I was thirteen and it was on a beach in France. I'd spotted this beautiful French boy the minute we arrived, and one night he talked to me at the hotel disco. I told him I was sixteen 'cause I figured that must've been his age. I had on this black dress with thin straps. I felt different when I was wearing it. Like a grown-up, I guess. We left the dance floor and went to the beach. The boy, I don't remember his name either actually, led me over to this white plastic sunlounger and then suddenly his tongue was all over my mouth. It was awful. A washing machine. Saliva everywhere. He hardly knew any Italian but he could say, "Can you lick?" And then, "Will you touch it a bit?"'

'God.'

'Yup.'

'Did you?'

'No!'

Joe slid down her body and rested his head on the jut of her hip, his breath hot puffs across her pelvis. She stroked his sweaty hair, massaging the scalp a little. He moaned softly. 'How about your first fuck?' he asked.

Her first time was at seventeen. How could she relay that experience? How he had ordered her around. Stand up. Take that off. Bend over. Try on top. *Relax relax relax.*

She shuddered.

'Painful. A boy from the neighbouring farm who treated me like a mare.'

'Jesus. What did he look like?'

'Gorgeous. Hair so black it was blue, dark brooding eyes. I'd crushed on him for months but was too scared to tell him, so I wrote all these letters, pages and pages, but never sent them. Then we got together. He was so disappointing in reality. I missed the intensity of wanting him from afar.' She sighed. 'It was such a shame, so much better when he wasn't interested.'

'You're so contrary.' Joe looked at her, smirking. He slid back up her body and rested his head on the side-swell of her breast.

'Fidget,' she murmured.

She hooked her leg into his and thought again of her childhood stuffed toy – her first fatal taste of unrequited affection. Could that explain why she felt so attached to her phone, the habitual swiping, lovingly staring into a screen which did not love her back? Lately, she liked to google Joe's name, listen repeatedly to a podcast he recorded years ago about Mod fashion. In fact she did this obsessively, on the bus or when she had enough energy to walk home from work, pushing her earphones in as far as they'd go so it was like he was talking directly into her ear. When the interviewer interjected with girlish flirting laughter, she rippled with jealousy. What he said wasn't so important. She had little time for fashion or nostalgia – especially a combination of the two. It was his voice, its cadences. On sleepless nights, Luca passed out beside her, she'd listen and take out the memory of Joe's body, turning it this way and that in her mind, recalling every touch. Sometimes it was exciting; sometimes it felt like sorrow. She'd get up and make a grilled cheese sandwich, catch herself mouthing odd words that had stuck in her head like: *tailored, six and seven, gab up, Levi's.*

'Do you remember that kind of teenage longing, where it actually physically hurts?' she asked him now.

'Yeah, but it wasn't with my first. That was the least romantic experience of my life.'

'Tell.'

'Raquel. I was fourteen. Pretty sure she had a boy-friend. She asked me which hole I wanted to put it in first.'

'Liar! Who says that?'

'Honest to God. It was in the bathroom of my sister's best friend's house. There was a party. Her mum was a hippie and didn't bat an eyelid at the stuff we used to get up to. Joop! – that was Raquel's perfume; she used to bathe herself in the stuff. Anyway, she lured me into the bathroom, she was sixteen – my sister's age – and I'd never even had a blowjob. I went from a snog and squeeze to full-blown shagging. I remember being really aware of how big I was and feeling too worried about hurting her to come.'

'You didn't come?'

'Nope. I faked it. Men do that too, you know. I ripped the johnny off my knob straight after and binned it so she couldn't see.'

She laughed. 'I thought most men come in seconds their first time.'

'Not most men, am I, darlin'? Anyway, we fooled around for a few weeks after that night, but then she started seeing some older guy from the college. I was gutted.'

'I don't know anyone who wasn't gutted the first time.'

'Is it weird that I want to know what the sex is like between you and Luca?'

'Yes,' she said, rolling over. Why did he always have to do that? He couldn't seem to help himself, like picking at the loose skin of a scab. She grabbed her tin of cigarettes from the bedside table and flicked the pink lid of Joe's Zippo. As she took the first drag, she listened to the fizz of the tip. 'Why do you have a Hello Kitty lighter anyway?'

'Open the balcony door if you're going to smoke,' he said.

She pulled the sheet from the floor and wrapped it around her. A burst of frosty air raced into the room. Sex with Luca wasn't bad, but every move was familiar. He was too well schooled in what she liked. It wasn't intimate any more. Inevitably, one of them remembered something the other needed to know about the kids as they were doing it. They both always came, but far away from each other. She could not bear how afterwards he kissed her whole body, lightly, chastely, with reverence. If only she could erase their history. She wanted to empty out to become a better vessel for new things. She was hungry for the new. A new touch, a new taste. The surprise at discovering someone else's hairy shoulders, or a superb kink in their penis. Joe had a fascination with navels. He would tongue hers and push in his thumb as far as it would go. She would watch, fascinated, vaguely thinking about belly fluff, before wriggling free and climbing on to his face. She could not get enough of his long straight nose.

Out on the balcony, the cold set into her skin. Below,

rush hour was in full effect. About now, Luca would be cooking the kids' dinner, filling the kitchen with too-loud discordant jazz, humming along as he stirred a crowd of pans on the hob. She longed to hear all about Lyddie's day at school, to find out if Freddy won his football match. There were so many things she loved about her life, but did she honour them? She pressed up against the balcony railing. It felt too thin to be effective. She tried to rattle it, test its strength. She imagined it breaking, her body falling in slow motion like a stray piece of laundry slipped from a washing line.

'The first time I did it with a girl I loved, well that was something else,' Joe said, joining her.

She didn't want to hear about anyone Joe had loved – those kinds of stories always had the same endings. What she really wanted was to learn about the first time he did heroin, but she'd given up asking. He refused to speak about the two years he'd lost. He stopped going to NA a while ago and had run dry of the impulse to share. It was morbid, but she wanted to know what a person went through when they gave themselves over to something so completely, how they found the strength to surrender it all and then come out on the other side.

He moved her hair and planted a kiss on the mole she hated on the back of her neck. 'The hair growing out of this thing is outrageous,' he said. 'Let me at it.' He pinched the skin and she elbowed him in the ribs.

'Don't be a jerk.'

'How are you a knockout even with a hairy mole?' he said, plucking the strand with his fingers.

Her skin smarted.

'All done.'

'Christ you're a dick.'

He smiled and took the cigarette from her mouth and pushed smoke rings into the dark. She watched them evaporate, swallowed up by the city night.

There was an hour left before she was expected home. Joe had dozed off, mouth hanging open. One arm was bent behind his head, fair hair sex-messed – miles from his careful Mod style. She ran her fingers along the outline of his abdominal muscles, counting the ribbony chest hairs which sprouted from his pale skin: there were eight. On his left side a creamy scar remained from a shady encounter. On the right a tattoo spelling L O V E in black ink, letters shaped like skywriting, spilled down his ribcage. She'd never liked that tattoo, couldn't figure out what love meant to him. His body was firm and smooth, lanky but with a fluidity to it like the cautious first lines an artist makes. It was the creases in his face which gave away his age, the jagged patterns across the forehead, deep crow's feet at the corners of his eyes, their rims red from a life spent smoking too much pot. His cheeks were red too – the burst blood vessels an unmistakable sign of a former hedonist. He'd retained the energy of an addict, cartwheeling from one thing to the next, a new interest or hobby. Now she thought about it, he was always ready to jack his load at the promise of the *new*. Maybe they had more in common than she liked to admit.

She stroked the length of his inner thigh, following the muscles down to his feet. He slept on. She retrieved the nail varnish from the bathroom, and then painted the first three toes of his left foot. She blew across them, laughing a little. The hotel's monogrammed terry robe was on the floor and she belted it around her. It was so soft, so exquisitely laundered. At home, she barely remembered to separate whites and colours. The whole household's jumpers were bobbled.

She got up and prowled around the suite. Everything had been strategically arranged. An empty cut-glass bowl, a tall vase filled with pungent white lilies, a few framed paintings – simple smudges and daubs of taupe – hanging on the walls. She pulled open the drawers and cupboards, hoping to uncover some object left behind by a previous occupant. A bracelet slipped from a wrist, a hair tie on the shower floor, a chamois cloth dropped by housekeeping in a hurry. But there was only an anonymous hairdryer and some extra blankets. The room was a blank slate, an empty canvas. An unreasonable freedom.

Under the guise of her working nights at the hospital, they'd been sneaking around for almost a year. Not only in hotel rooms: Joe had a host of rich friends who spent weekends away – Côte d'Azur, Palma Majorca, Cap Ferret. Their cats would need feeding or plants watering and Joe, with that alluring grin of his, would offer up his services. People liked him. They warmed themselves on his feverish energy, were drawn in as he leaned imperceptibly closer, eyes widening, head cocked to the right as he listened, pouring his attention on them. He had the habit of sucking in the fleshy part of his cheeks, making his bottom lip jut out to look both petulant and sweet.

Little did Joe's friends and colleagues know how they fucked on their kitchen tables, in their expansive hallways, rolling across living-room floors on thick Moroccan carpets, on every well-made, over-cushioned bed. The first time she'd watched him put a key into the lock to open the front door, it felt more intimate than anything else they'd done together. She learned to look away.

Each home-owner would invariably leave a thank-you bottle of Billecart, or Beluga caviar in the fridge, which they'd consume in a hot bath. She liked to walk around the houses half as if she owned them, half as a prospective buyer. Opening and closing melamine cabinets, tapping walls. She'd slip into a stranger's silk dressing gown to smoke on the terrace. Mist the air with a musky rose or oud to cover the smell of sex. The only place she wouldn't venture into was children's bedrooms.

She'd seen pockets of London previously unknown to her this way, ferried about in cabs. It was her favourite feeling, being alone in the back of a cab musing on an imminent fuck. The landscaped gardens of Kensal Rise terraces, wall-to-wall concrete of Peckham flats. There were a few places they'd gone back to. The converted church at Cadogan Gardens, all velvet and red textured wallpaper, taxidermy bats hanging in the stairway, a python shifting in its cage by the huge front door. Lucian Freud, Gilbert and George, and Francis Bacon graced the walls. No matter where they went, she always looked at the art first, felt better about the place if she could see its owners had good taste.

She liked the loft in Clerkenwell best. It belonged to one of Joe's old musician buddies. There was something about the area – beautiful grand old buildings but an in-between kind of space, mostly used as a stop-gap for people working in the City, not quite as cool as its neighbouring areas further east. She'd spat out her wine when Joe told her what the rent was. She could see why his friend had fallen for the loft, though, its oak panelling, high ceilings with cast-iron windows, elaborate bulbous light sculptures. He always left porterhouse steaks in the fridge for Joe, thick fleshy slabs of rump, a little marbled fat – no bone. Joe would generously douse them in rock salt, heat a griddle pan until it smoked then throw on the meat, blood forming little pools in the corner. It sizzled and spat. They'd eat them rare, standing up in the kitchen, always ravenous.

But the problem with eating your fill was no longer feeling hungry.

In the otherwise empty bedside table drawer was a Gideon's Bible. Amazed this tradition still existed, she picked it up and turned the rough red leatherette cover in her hands, admiring how it rebelled against the hotel colour scheme, how its contents contradicted the way the room was used. She unfastened the gold-plated stud from her left ear and slipped it between the crêpe pages. Something to say she had been here.

Joe's eyes opened as she was setting the Bible back in place. 'Little late for your Catholic guilt to kick in, darlin'.' He winked.

The wink was too much. She wanted to tell him he was a rat, a dirty rat, sneaking around with his best friend's wife. But she was the wife, the rat, the sneak. He was looking at his painted toenails. 'Cheeky minx!' he said, laughing.

She took a breath. It was all so easy for him. She knew she was jealous more than angry. How had he made it to thirty-eight without accruing a single responsibility? He tore a piece of skin from his foot then looked up and smiled, unaware. She shook her head at him. He slipped out of the sheets, slowly, one lean leg at a time, picked her up, his dick half hard again, prodding her thigh, and laid her gently on the bed. He rolled on to his side and gazed at her. 'Sorry,' he said. 'That wasn't very sensitive.'

She shrugged, leaned across him and checked her small gold watch lying on the table. The cheese sandwich was still on his breath. 'Thirty minutes.'

'How you fixed for next Thursday?'

'Lyddie has a school play.'

'Friday?'

'It's Valentine's.'

'Ooh la la. Week after?'

She didn't have the words. The shadowy light of the bedside lamp turned Joe's face butter-pale. In the beginning, in the first spark of the new, the risk always felt worth it. She couldn't survive on toast alone – she had to have the butter. So now she reached for Joe and, although she was spent and sore, she gave that fuck everything she had because she knew it was going to be the last. The last.

She missed the moment even as it was happening.

Outside was freezing. In the cobbled lane where his Vespa was parked, Joe raked back her hair and carefully placed a helmet over her head, pushing down so the foam lining moulded to the sides. He looked very serious as he fixed the buckle under her chin until he said, 'On ya get, love,' and patted the leather seat. She rolled her eyes, then swung a leg over and waited as he adjusted his chinos and slid in front. He swivelled and to the side of her face said, 'Shall I drop you at the top end of the park?' She nodded and pulled her gloves from her coat pocket, shoving her hands inside the thick grey wool.

He turned the ignition and the bassy sound of the engine bounced off the brick buildings. From inside the padding of her helmet, it sounded like the ocean's echo in one of the shells Lyddie collected and kept on her windowsill. She wrapped her arms around Joe's middle and breathed in the peaty scent of his leather jacket, tracing its cracks and veins with her fingers. They set off, and the wind lifted up her hair. She became curiously aware of her neck, that patch of exposed skin Joe had kissed earlier. It suddenly occurred to her she'd have to explain to Luca why her toenails were painted, how she found the time during a nursing conference.

Being on the back of the Vespa was always unsettling. It reminded her of when she was nineteen, scooting around Veneto in the summer, a rucksack of red wine on her back, cigarette half-slipping from her mouth. She'd pick up Luca from the farm and they'd drive out to a field somewhere. Grass stains, come stains, berry-red mouths. They'd carved their initials into the bark of a cypress tree that one time neither of them had remembered to bring a condom.

Another life ago.

Tall trees lined the Knightsbridge roads. They were positioned with equal spaces between them, alert and watchful, like the Buckingham Palace guards close by. The Vespa's tyres bounced across the craters of cobblestones and she liked the feel of the engine beneath her, the percussive pulse of it. The sky was cloudless, the nearly full moon only managing a faint glow in the chaos of city lights.

The air was sharp as Joe picked up speed. The small streets converged into one long silver thread and soon Embankment loomed before them: the London Eye, Waterloo bridge, Blackfriars bridge, Southwark bridge, all strung with delicate yellow lights like ship sails. On the right, a tangle of houseboats bobbed as they rode the dark brown water of the Thames. Cars swarmed around them and Joe weaved in and out of the traffic so that the other vehicles became a blur of headlights.

For the last few months, she'd had a recurring dream where Joe would be driving his Vespa, turn a sharp right and she would let go, just to see what would happen, and then fall off, abandoned to the night. Joe never noticed, carried on driving, and to her surprise, she wouldn't smash on to the asphalt but instead float up and away, soon forgetting all about him. As she would drift behind the thin white trail of the Vespa's exhaust, there wasn't any noise except the wind as it cut through the night, her legs paddling air, bones like water, buildings billowing as she passed, kicking up towards an endless conveyor belt of clouds. She'd swim into a pleasing electric current, welcoming, having no idea where she was going, or how long it would take to get there, her skin tingling, legs thrashing about wildly, her wedding band and C-section scar missing. But then she'd be jolted out of the dream, panting, on the verge of coming, only to open her eyes and be greeted by the familiar outline of Luca's body in the dark, his chest rising and falling, sound asleep.

The line of beech trees around Victoria Park loomed ahead now. She leaned in and asked Joe to circle a couple of times before he dropped her off. Just five more minutes, she told herself, and then she'd wake up.

March

Sharing Time

When Vicky's son had been in hospital for a month, her sister, Beverley, moved in. They hadn't lived together for twenty-seven years. In the evenings, they watched repeats of eighties detective dramas until the early hours. They often ate ice cream for dinner. Beverley put a stop to Vicky sleeping in her son's room so for the last five months they'd shared her double bed. At night, Vicky lay awake, listening to Beverley's snores, the twitch of her heavy legs beneath the covers.

This morning, like every morning, she showered, oiled her body, put on clean clothes. She powdered her face, coated each of her pale lashes with black, rubbed a pink balm into her lips. She joined the traffic which stretched along the three-mile route to the hospital. Homerton High Street, Wick Road. She always held her breath as she turned on to Victoria Park Road, but chose not to avoid it. The beech trees sagged with rain. Pink and white blossoms were carried away by the wind. She turned on the radio to drown out the windscreen wipers.

At Raven Row, she paid for parking. The hospital's blue glass building was seventeen storeys. Whenever she felt panicky, she sat in her car and counted them – bottom to top, top to bottom.

She didn't need to ask for directions any more. The corridors all looked the same, but it was a maze she'd cracked. The canteen ladies kept her almond milk in their fridge. She greeted everyone by first name. They replied in kind. *Hi, Victoria, Morning, Victoria, All right, Victoria – make sure you're getting some rest.*

At nine a.m., the whole hospital gleamed. Her son's bed was at the end of the ward next to the window. Vicky stepped into his bay. His body was motionless beneath the sheets. Each time she saw him, she heard Beverley's voice: *At least they didn't get his face.* 'Hello, baby,' Vicky said, stroking his forehead. 'Ready to wake up yet?' She said the same thing every morning, hoping he'd learn through repetition. His eyes stayed shut, but she could hear him breathing faintly above the sound of the monitors, above the murmured conversations of nurses and patients.

On the days when his college friends visited, they stood by the bed, unsure where to look, unsure of what to do. They were shocked by the state of his hands and neck, the parts of his chest exposed by his gown. Vicky would ask them to talk, tell stories. She was clingy with his friends she'd already met, worse with the ones who were strangers. She was desperate for clues about his life outside of their home. She knew he was outspoken, hyperactive, a ball of energy. But she discovered he drank much more than she thought he did. That he had two girls in tow, both younger than him. Neither had come to visit. She took this personally. No one could tell her what he was doing in the park that day, so no matter how many times she went back to that morning, she still could not imagine ways to prevent it from happening. Guilt was stuck on a loop, like the train track he played with as a toddler.

The details she did know haunted her: he ran from his attacker, and the dazzling pain sent him flying backwards over a bench. Hands protecting face, then clutching torso. The thud of head on kerb. Left arm bent beneath and broken. Out cold. Three or four seconds of blind panic; five months in a coma and counting.

When the police came to her nursery she'd dropped the tray of afternoon snacks. The floor was a mess of yogurt and fruit. The officer said acid can be used in robberies, burglaries, revenge attacks, during thefts of mopeds, or to intimidate witnesses. It can be used on spurned lovers, during domestic disputes, in acts of religious or racial hatred. *Please think hard*, they urged her. *Does he have the latest iPhone? Does he attend college? Who are his friends? Is there anyone who might have a vendetta against him? Is he involved in any gangs? Is he known to take or deal drugs?* What they were really enquiring was: how well do you know your son? Implied: did he have this coming to him? She stood there, quiet. Finally she asked, *Who is the suspect here?*

'Morning, Victoria,' a nurse said, breezing in with a clipboard. She was a locum and Vicky couldn't remember her name, but appreciated the woman had learned hers. The nurse checked the tubes, his blood pressure, and emptied his catheter. Vicky didn't look away. She knew her son's body better than she had in a decade.

To his right, separated only by a thin blue curtain, was Naomi's daughter. She'd been in hospital even longer than Vicky's son. She could hear her waking up, greeting the nurse and asking for water. Vicky would do anything to hear her son's voice, for his eyes to flip open, for him to sit bolt upright in bed, say, *All right, Mum? Where am I?* In short, she wanted a Hollywood ending. In reality, the longer he was here, the less likely he was to wake and be able to say anything at all. He'd never scored more than a six on the Glasgow Coma Scale. She spent hours waiting for something to happen anyway. Time outside the hospital was too thick, too slow, too full of worry.

Vicky and Naomi had sat side by side for months. They'd seen dozens of people come and go. They'd shared the soundtrack of puking, wailing, sniffling, emergency alarms activated. It had been quieter in the ICU, but they both agreed that the routine of the ward was preferable. Vicky liked to think that she and Naomi were united by their strength, but she suspected the glue was their fear.

She'd given up her job at the nursery when the compassionate leave ran out. She packed a box of her things: aluminium water bottle, four Tupperware with three mismatched lids, folders of craft materials. She stole several pots of PVA glue, the kind with a paint stick attached to the lid, and a twelve-by-twelve scrapbook album, forty white pages. She peeled off the ACID AND LIGNIN FREE sticker on its cover. She took out a loan.

'Keep up your interests,' Naomi had urged. 'Find new ones.' So Vicky read medical papers on brain trauma, articles on Generation Z masculinity. She joined online forums for coma survival patients. She knew it wasn't what Naomi meant at all. They were useless activities, attempting to unwind time, to ping it back to being linear. Only occasionally would she give up and surf her usual beauty forums, gorge herself on make-up tutorials. She searched for the best deals on city breaks, planned dozens of trips, and then stopped at the page prompting her to enter card details.

She looked up statistics. The UK had one of the highest rates of acid attacks in the world. In London, the worst year for attacks saw 465 recorded. There had been a consistent rise in the number of alt-right sites and blogs which linked acid attacks to Muslims, Asians and migrants. But only six per cent of all suspects in London over the last fifteen years were Asian. First she was surprised by the existence of her own prejudice, and then she was filled with rage. The number 465 buzzed in her head. Her son, only one of hundreds of victims out there. Did they have anything in common?

So she began scrapbooking. It was a routine of sorts. She'd open a bottle of lager, listen to the hiss of gas escape. Sometimes she read the papers; sometimes she searched online and printed her findings. She was careful as she cut. The snip of scissors as they sliced through paper, the faint tang of glue as she stuck them on to the page. She filed away the details, storing them so she could cross-reference each case, so that they'd keep out of the folds of her brain where they might linger and burn.

An aspiring model and her cousin were sprayed with acid through their car window. On social media, the attack was labelled a hate crime conducted by white supremacists against Muslims. No evidence was found that this was the case. The attacker handed himself in two weeks later, confessing to hearing voices in his head.

The back of the scrapbook was for clippings about her son. Updates about new leads; stories about the lack of updates. There was nothing recent.

Somewhere on the ward an emergency alarm was activated. Outside was grey and wet. In the half-light of his bay she asked him, 'Does it hurt? Are we managing your pain?' There was a time when plasters and Savlon had made it all better. She still carried both in her handbag.

At ten a.m., Nina did the checks. She was the most palatable nurse on the ward. Talia was so nice that Vicky couldn't bear talking to her. She preferred Nina because she was decidedly unsympathetic. She had cropped black hair, a blunt fringe, and was direct to the point of impatience. Plus she smoked. She'd once found Vicky weeping in the car park, slumped in her seat, legs half in, half out of her car, and removed her cigarette from her mouth to say, 'Music can help. We had a woman who played her husband's favourite songs every day. It helped connect her to him. Use the playlists from his phone.'

His iPhone had never been recovered, but Nina didn't know that. Vicky found his iPad in the second drawer of his bedside table. She scrolled through Spotify, locating the most recently played. She discovered he only listened to hip-hop. She couldn't follow the lyrics, couldn't distinguish between artists. So she educated herself. In total, she and Beverley watched fifteen hours of a history of rap series on Netflix. Beverley made proper popcorn in a saucepan on the hob. Each time a kernel hit the glass lid, Vicky winced. They slathered the lot in melted butter and salt flakes and then ate it in place of dinner.

She hadn't known that Tupac's mother was a Black Panther. She listened to the song 'Brenda's Got a Baby' on repeat until she couldn't stop shaking at the thought of giving birth alone on a bathroom floor. In an old magazine article she found online, Tupac talked about whether he considered it to be a political song. She read the article twice, trying to feel closer to her son, but the only part she could remember was Tupac's statement that one person's problems can affect a whole community. How it's usually the innocent ones who get hurt.

She checked the iPad's history. It was full of wrestling porn. She watched the videos for an entire hour, thrilled and full of lust, before she deleted the thread. She waited for the shame to kick in but it didn't. Her cheeks flushed with heat. Her body was too responsive.

This morning, she sat through thirty-five minutes of hip-hop as she read the day's papers aloud. She was more informed about the outside world than she'd ever been. The irony of this was not lost on her. The headline: FORMER UN CLIMATE ENVOY JOINS AN EVER-GROWING LIST OF EXPERTS FRUSTRATED BY BRITAIN'S LACK OF LEADERSHIP ON CARBON EMISSIONS. She twirled the now long tufts of her son's hair around her fingers as she read. He'd like it this long. The next page was about the latest boom in Sri Lankan restaurants, where to find a good kottu roti in London. In the background, Monie Love and Queen Latifah were rapping about the power of being a woman. Vicky had grown quite fond of them, but as the song ended she decided to cheat and select her own playlist. 'Sorry, baby,' she said, touching her nose to his forehead. Blur, then Elastica, then Suede blared out. She remembered fucking to Pulp's 'Sheffield: Sex City' with his father one night. Red-wine calm, warm skin, the marble wing of his hipbones.

She woke from a nap when Nina began the midday checks. She'd stopped wearing a watch, and observed Nina's sequence of time gratefully.

Nina froze and turned to look at Vicky. 'His right foot moved away from my hand. Just slightly, an inch, maybe.'

Vicky stood and the iPad clattered to the floor. 'When?'

'Just now.'

'Further than last time?'

'Yes. It could be nothing, but it could be a localized response. I'm going to tell the consultant.' She left the ward.

To no one Vicky said, 'Stay calm. Stay calm. Stay calm.'

A nurse went to visit her daughter's grave. She sat on a bench to rest and reflect. Nearby, a dispute about drugs was taking place. A bottle fell to the ground and was kicked away. The liquid hit the woman's face, arms, upper body and lower legs. Eleven days later, she died of sepsis relating to her burns.

All of Vicky's energy was spent holding herself upright, arms folded across chest, fingertips digging into flesh, trying to ignore the smell of ammonia, trying not to lean into a future, because what a betrayal hope had become.

Nina returned. 'It could be hours before the consultant's free. There's been an accident, a motorway pile-up on the A12. We'll keep monitoring him for any more changes.'

Time passed. Vicky fell into a deep exhaustion, as if trying to reach her son in sleep.

'Knock knock,' Naomi joked before pulling the curtain aside. She was clasping a tinfoil package shaped like the neck of a swan. 'Flapjacks,' she said, with her soft, liquid voice. 'Rocky-road topping.'

Vicky was surprised to find it was still lunchtime.

Naomi worked for a catering company. Her clothes smelled of the outside world: baked bread, fried potatoes, caramelized sugar. She was petite, toned, and always looked attractive – perhaps because her skin was glowy, or maybe because she always brought food.

They'd made a pact that remembrance should not become a catalogue of losses. But in hushed tones they dished the dirt on the fathers. The ones who didn't stick around. Vicky almost loved Naomi because she was tender and friendly and her daughter was on her way out and Vicky's son still might wake up and oh God oh God it felt good not being the one who was worse off for once.

She was too hopeful to tell Naomi about her son's foot. What if she was punished for her excitement and jinxed it? So she swallowed down the news. They sat and talked intermittently on the blue plastic chairs positioned between the two beds. Naomi's daughter was asleep with headphones in: white, wireless buds a too-bright extension of her jaundiced ears.

'Weirdest thing he ever put in his mouth as a kid?' Naomi asked. 'Hers was a Sylvanian Families figure. Remember those?'

'When he was four he was obsessed with licking washing powder,' Vicky replied. 'I found him in the laundry cupboard, clutching a box of suds to his chest, licking his fingers. When I asked why, he said, *I wanted to know how clean tastes.*'

Stray oats fell from Naomi's lips as she listened. She was wearing textured workout leggings and the flakes gathered in the webbing.

'When he was thirteen, he went vegan for a year. Mealtimes were so tricky I almost hated him,' Vicky confessed. 'But then I'd remember how when he was little, he told me that he'd grow up and marry me. And I'd forgive him.'

They discussed recipes. 'I'll make jalapeño cornbread tomorrow,' Vicky said. 'We holidayed in Cancún when he was fifteen. He loved the food. Stomach like an ox.'

Vicky hoped food smells could be the thing that woke him all the way up. Smell was as important as sound, the consultant had said.

'As a baby, he'd smell like sweet oat milk from the baths I gave him for eczema,' she told Naomi, straying off topic. 'Then one day, he was all Lynx Africa. Eucalyptus from his spot gel.'

This came out as a rush of words, too fast.

When the flapjacks were finished, Naomi kissed her daughter's forehead and left for work. Vicky drew the curtain around her son. She wondered whether to shave his stubbly cheeks. So far, she'd left that to the nurses, afraid of nicking the flesh. She pulled back the sheets, examined his thighs – the source of his multiple grafts, covered now with great swathes of livid skin. Dr Kraicer had told her the prolonged coma did him a favour. With Vicky's consent, they could perform the necessary skin grafts while he was unconscious and skip the painful recovery. 'And,' the junior doctor continued, 'when he wakes up, the skin will already be healing.'

'When?'

'What?'

'When will he wake up?'

He flashed a desperate look at the consultant.

She gave her consent.

She knew they'd used a scalpel, but she'd imagined the surgeon cutting the skin with scissors – like she does with news stories – using neat controlled snips. In her mind, they'd pasted the squares of smooth skin with glue that looked just like PVA. The nurses covered the borrowed spots with Kaltostat, a seaweed-like dressing to help stop any bleeding, and on top went a large padded gauze covered with wool and bandages. The whole lot stayed there for two weeks. The Kaltostat acted as an artificial scab for him, becoming stiffer with time. This was, apparently, a more painful sensation than the wound itself. He'd never know. She'd imagined it as being covered in plaster of Paris, feeling it tighten unbearably around her legs as she tried to walk.

She bent to rest her head against the healed patches. 'You are an excellent runner,' she told his legs, feeling her own warm breath return to her. 'My God you are fast. Do you remember sports day last year at college? You were a whir around that huge track. I couldn't get a seat close enough to the front to photograph it.' She took out her phone to watch an old blurry video of that day, as if to confirm it really happened, but she couldn't watch for more than a few seconds.

Her son's legs were long and lean like her own. She

picked up a bottle of lotion, tipping the white cream into her hands, and massaged his calves with antibacterial moisturizer. She took extra care with his feet. She had to believe that he could feel her touch the same way she knew he heard her voice reading to him in the womb. His toenails needed clipping. She fetched nail scissors from his toiletry bag. White half-moons fell on the linoleum.

Sleet hit the ward's window. She sighed. She was silently cheering on the explosion of spring. She wanted things in the earth to wake up, to turn green. She trained her gaze on his body, waiting for it to move again. 'Why would you move for Nina, and not for me?' she whispered venomously. 'Please,' she added. 'It's time.' Then she apologized, gently touching the skin on his torso and neck, the places where it had hardened. It felt like cracked soil after months of drought, like bark. Even after all the grafts, there was nothing soft, or lifelike about it. The skin was unrecognizable. It didn't belong to her boy. It had more in common with the park.

A two-year-old boy suffered burns to his face when acid was thrown while he was sitting in his pushchair in a park. His mother and father, who had been taking the toddler for a walk, were also hurt. The boy recovered, with partial burns to his face. Nobody has ever been arrested.

Nina returned. 'He's going to be a while,' she said of the consultant. She looked at Vicky's son. 'We've got him on obs every fifteen minutes.'

Vicky stared at her blankly.

'You should give yourself a break. It's not good to be this tense. You know what happened last time. If anything changes we'll call you.'

Vicky ran a finger across her son's brow to smooth the hairs down. Then she nodded and, although reluctant, kissed her son's cheek, inhaled his sour exhale, and left.

Outside, the weather was like a wet washcloth pressed against her skin. She pulled up her hood and ran to the car. As she drove, she mentally raided the fridge and decided to make carrot and ginger soup. At lunchtime, the journey took ten minutes. She navigated recklessly through the quiet streets. Leaves hit the windscreen. It hadn't stopped raining all month. Her clothes smelled damp even when they were dry.

At home, Beverley was at the kitchen table, typing on her laptop. Vicky resented how she didn't even need to go into her office, how her sister's children were grown and in university, living their lives. She called out hello but then saw her scrapbook on the table. She must have forgotten to put it back behind the cookbooks. Beverley looked up at her and said, 'What *is* this?'

'That's mine.'

Beverley shook her head slowly, sadly. 'I don't get it. Are you trying to make yourself feel better? Feel worse?'

Vicky swallowed. 'I'm trying to understand who gets attacked. The different types of people. There'll be patterns between cases, things that link them. It's easier to see when they're all stuck in one place.'

Beverley closed the book. 'It's just... a bit sick, Vicky.'

'I'm trying to understand.' She stopped, waiting for a response. 'I need answers,' Vicky continued, louder this time. 'There's so much I don't know.' She heard her voice go up another notch.

She opened the fridge, gathered a handful of carrots, and peeled them methodically over the bin. As she chopped, she recalled all the times in her life that Beverley had pissed her off. When they were small, the silent pinching in dark cinemas with their mum; the way she pretended not to know her at school; how she flirted with Vicky's first boyfriend; how condescending she'd been when Vicky gave birth, how she'd almost gloated over Vicky doing it alone. Not that Beverley's marriage lasted the course. She added the ginger and remembered every single piece of patronizing advice Beverley had ever doled out.

And then she remembered that first month when Beverley moved in and had to bathe her. Her sister had always been much bigger, with strong, wide thighs, but she managed to sit on the edge of the tub, and she sang the same songs their mother used to sing, and the water slid off Vicky's back, warm and cleansing.

'Lunch is ready,' she called out, her voice strained.

They ate in silence until Beverley said, 'You're losing your figure. You're all skin and bones.' She got up, found the iPad, and downloaded a fitness app, paying for the Home Transformation Guide. They watched the intro video. Vicky stared at the young trainer's skin, tanned and smooth and blemish-free. Her abs were so defined they looked drawn on. She felt good at the prospect of exercising again: she could be energetic, quick, nimble – like her son. Like her son had been. They cleared a space in the living room, and Vicky rolled out her yoga mat. They collapsed into a fit of giggles trying to do burpees.

Sweating on the floor and staring up at the ceiling, she told Beverley that he moved his foot this morning. There was a pause and then Beverley thanked God in a suppressed but urgent manner that Vicky found very worrying. She'd never heard her sister address any kind of God before. It took away from the moment, and she was frightened again, of false alarms, of hope dried up.

Afterwards, Vicky settled into an armchair, put on her son's headphones, and tuned into her favourite true-crime podcast. She rested her phone on the arm of the chair in case the hospital called, and then relaxed as the presenter's voice rushed into her ears with other people's problems. The sound quality was so good that she once googled the brand of headphones and discovered they cost two hundred pounds. She had no idea where her son found that kind of money. She decided to leave that thought there.

There was no phone call from the hospital.

The boyfriend of a reality TV star threw acid across an east London club. He wounded twenty people. His defence was that he thought the bottle contained a liquid date-rape drug which he had snatched from two men after overhearing them plan to spike a girl's drink. He was sentenced to twenty years in prison.

Early evening, she drove back to demand news from the consultant. Beverley wanted to join her, but when her son's left eye had flickered Beverley came with her and then nothing changed. So Vicky said she'd go alone, thank you very much. She was stuck in traffic for a long time and when she moved through the last set of lights, dusk had happened.

The hospital looked larger at night, more geometric. A different beast. Talia was on duty. Her hair was swept up on to the top of her head and teased into the shape of a bow. She told Vicky the consultant was still busy with the car-collision victims. 'He hasn't made it on to the ward yet,' she said, 'but he'll come as soon as he can.' Vicky glared at Talia. She could wring her neck. She could almost hear it crack. She blamed Talia personally for the hold-up. 'I'll wait for him,' she told her defiantly, though what she was defying really, she didn't know. Talia gave her a half-smile. 'It could be a couple of hours,' she said.

Naomi returned to the ward after her catering job finished. She gave Vicky a hot chocolate from the vending machine at the other end of the hall. They blew across their cups and sipped, taking turns to divulge the irritating things their children did. There was the usual litany of gripes: wet towels left on the floor, cotton rounds flushed not thrown and the drainpipes clogged. Vicky said, 'I've never seen anyone take more pleasure in burping. He loves to let it rip. You know when they're newborns and pass gas with their whole body? He's still like that – it rolls up through his stomach and out of his mouth.'

Naomi laughed.

'And when he was fifteen, he started thanking me for telling him off. I'd hold up his mud-stained running kit he'd just dumped on the floor, and say something like, *You know, I wasn't born just to pick up after your mess*, and he'd reply, *Thank you for telling me, Mum*, with this unbearable smirk on his face.'

When Naomi fell asleep, Vicky went to the nurses' station. They were laughing. Before she could open her mouth, Talia put down her lip balm, tucked a flyaway hair behind her ear and told Vicky that the consultant would be there as soon as he could. 'Go stretch your legs,' Talia said. 'Get some air.'

Vicky nodded; she'd go for a walk, but she had no intention of leaving the building. It was so easy to wander anywhere in the hospital at night. All corridors were fair game. She slipped through doors in the sticky delay before they properly closed. She liked the grey, functional store cupboards, the way they were divided by ailments. The occupational therapy and physiotherapy rooms were always empty and smelled like hand sanitizer. She took a seat in the relatives' lounge, stared at the magnolia walls. A pink silk orchid bothered her to distraction – if a real orchid couldn't survive in hospital then what could?

She headed downstairs to A & E to spy on the traumas. A balding man with a bleeding head was drinking from a paper bag. An elderly woman in a thin yellow dress was crying, her husband whispering into her ear. Four teenagers, eyes trained on one phone, silently watched something unfold, mouths agog. They were all lucky to have minor injuries – to not be crumbling day by day, week by week, personality hidden away, morphing and shifting beneath the eyelids. She didn't stay there long. The memory of the day of the attack rose to the surface, and she could see her own body in the rows of people waiting. But that couldn't be right: they hadn't had to wait.

When she returned to the ward, Naomi was crying. It didn't happen often any more but when the gates went down it was a flood. Vicky comforted her, feeling smug and capable until her own eyes began to brim.

Naomi left. There was still no sign of the consultant. She itched with impatience. Talia was too busy to stop and talk, so Vicky settled in the chair by her son's bed, all her nerves fired up, alert, watching for movement. Behind his body was the window: the smack of rain, and ambulance lights flashing blue and then disappearing. She listened to the hum of machines and could almost hear the tick of minutes as they passed: each one lost to him. Another, then another, then one more.

April

Counting Down

Three times a week, when he came to Bettie for English lessons, Daniel managed to be fifteen minutes late. So when she handed him the practice exam paper and he scribbled BLAH BLAH BLAH across its cover, they were already behind and Bettie was too tired to even despair.

'Daniel?'

No response.

She tried again, stringing out the syllables of his name like a lullaby. 'Dan-yal?' Her voice echoed in the classroom, a brief interruption from the whirring fan and buzzing halogen strip light. Its glare drew out the shadows under Daniel's eyes, made a halo of his bleached tips.

He'd been removed from the Pupil Referral Unit's regular classes. There was a fight, this time over a pair of trainers, and Bettie was supposed to be his punishment. He was too apathetic to kick up a fuss. It was his second week of after-school one-to-one tuition. There was one week left. Only a month until he'd sit the GCSE English exam.

She was sitting on top of the filing cabinet, her legs not quite reaching the worn brown carpet. The cabinet was old, stuffed years ago with someone else's yellowing papers. It often spilled its guts of its own accord, the middle two drawers swinging out, exposing spelling tests and punctuation exercises. She didn't have the energy to tidy it.

The whole classroom was a structural afterthought, about as big as Mia's art studio, with only a vast sheet of MDF to separate it from the home economics room. The smell of burnt cake, along with moans of frustration, often made its way through the partition. A bookcase lined one wall, its shelves buckling under rows of rec-ommended reading and out-of-date textbooks. Most of the spines had been broken, covers ripped off. This month's Literacy Goals, and posters made by past stu-dents, curling at the corners, clung to the walls with old Blu-tack. Laminated inspirational quotes the previous teacher had put up were dotted around the room.

Live as if you were to die tomorrow. Learn as if you were to live forever.

GANDHI

When she was first shown around the building, the deputy head told Bettie that her predecessor was off for six months before the statutory sick pay ran out. 'Depression,' she whispered conspiratorially. 'Either you can take it or you can't in this line of work, right? We've had a hard time finding the right person for the position. You're not a crier, are you? The supply teachers spent a lot of time in the disabled loo. The kids are bad but the coffee is good.'

She'd lied. The coffee was terrible.

If you don't like something, change it. If you can't change it, change your attitude.

MAYA ANGELOU

This one was affixed to a generic photo of a sunrise, the pixels stretched and fuzzy. It was a touching and redundant gesture – the only things these students were looking at were their phones.

'It's not gonna happen for me today,' Daniel said, shaking his head.

'He speaks. What's not going to happen?'

'Lessons. I can't focus with all the shit I got going on at home. Can I go to the art room and do my time there? Anika's been showing me some new stuff.'

Bettie dropped down from the filing cabinet with a thud. Her slacks were stuck to her thighs and she re-tucked her shirt into her waistband. She pulled up a chair and sat across from him. 'The thing about this room,' she said, resting her elbows on the table, 'is that you come here to do English and then you do English. It's reliable like that.'

He rolled his eyes and produced a bottle of Lucozade and a crumpled Greggs bag with a pink iced bun peeking out. She decided to ignore the classroom's no-eating rule. Either he was genuinely hungry or daring her to forbid it and start a time-wasting back and forth. He slumped back in his chair. The cheap plastic sagged.

He bit into the bun. 'You know I'm the man of my house, right? I should be out earning right now.'

'There's plenty of time for that after the exams.'

'What's the point? I'm going to get an apprenticeship on Savile Row like Alexander McQueen did before he got famous.'

She stifled a sigh. Daniel was a good kid but he was exhausting. There was no way he'd even be considered for an apprenticeship without maths or English GCSE. But he wouldn't hear it. The blind confidence of some teenage boys still had the ability to astound her. What would it be like if Mia ended up having one? She'd never wanted children, but it meant everything to Mia, and Mia meant everything to Bettie. If their second round of IVF worked, then everything would change, and she'd slip further away from the life she'd fought so hard to make. She acknowledged the thought then let it float away like she'd been learning to do at meditation classes.

'Here,' she said, passing Daniel another exam paper. 'I've tons of copies so do your worst.'

She retreated to her desk. Her nerves were still shot from the morning. The first lesson had been an hour of tantrums and defiance which culminated in a chair-throwing session miraculously broken up by the home economics teacher who terrified the kids with her unflappable niceness. It had been so embarrassing, to be rescued that way. The culprits were a group of angry fourteen-year-olds who'd been put in the same class by a chronic lack of foresight from the admin office. In the following lesson, the classroom's world globe narrowly missed her head after she pulled the plug on the MacBook when a kid tried to access the Dark Web. The paperwork this afternoon was going to be a nightmare.

'It's too hot,' Daniel said, crumpling the scribbled exam paper into a ball and hurling it in the direction of the bin. He dropped his pen on the floor and did not pick it up.

He was right. After a solid month of rain, it was a disconcertingly warm afternoon. She passed him another paper and rolled a biro towards him. He caught it and began to write on the table.

'You know they make these wipe-clean for exactly that reason,' she said, gesturing at a box of tissues.

Daniel stared at her and then grabbed one, rubbing it across a blue D and A. He opened the booklet, glanced at its pages, and then closed it. 'You look beat, Bettie. Don't you wish you were at home with your feet up? I got my nan a foot-spa thing for Christmas and she swears by it.'

'Just you wait till you get to my age. It won't seem so old.'

He gave her a look as if to say *I'm never going to be as old as you*, then reopened the booklet. Bettie let out her breath and sank her hands deep into her trouser pockets. Last lesson of the day. One more day of the week. Three months until summer break.

'What's the point of these again?' He gestured at the newspaper articles in the paper before him.

'To comment on their use of language and how they present the information on the page. You know this.'

'This article's rank.'

'Remind me?'

'About an acid attack in Bristol.'

'Oh yeah, I remember that one. Without reading the text, how can you tell the point of view of the journalist? Are they sympathetic? Are they neutral? Have they got an agenda?'

'Not a mind reader.'

'Look at the headline and the photo they chose to go with it.'

'It says, ACID ATTACK DROVE VICTIM TO EUTHANASIA. There's a photo of a white kid in a field.'

'Victim or perpetrator?'

'Victim. It'd be better if they showed his mash-up face,

if you ask me. Get the sympathy vote. Have they caught the attacker from last year yet? The Vicky Park guy?'

'I don't think so, no. You read about that?'

'I was in the park the day after it happened. It was creepy as fuck. No one was about. Fuckin' shocking, isn't it, that you can just be walking down the street and someone can chuck something at you that'll change your life forever. And you can buy that stuff anywhere.'

Daniel fell quiet. He was chewing the top of his pen, and a sliver of plastic stuck to his bottom lip. His nails were nicotine-stained and deep frown lines ran across his forehead. It was his third attempt to sit through a whole exam paper and this was the closest he'd ever got to engaging with the subject matter. She glanced at his work. Reading upside down, the wrong answers danced across the page in a line-defying scrawl. He didn't have a chance come exam time.

'Can't believe they haven't nicked anyone over that. Mum got done for one tiny burglary and got two years. Two years. Not even aggregated.'

Bettie just nodded. Daniel's keyworker had told the school his mum was being released soon.

'Can I do question three in bullet points?' Daniel asked.

'Nope.'

'Jesus.'

'Why are you always so surprised that you have to write in an English exam?'

'I'm an optimist. You should try it.'

'You think I'd be here if I wasn't?'

'Maybe you're a masochist.'

She laughed. Was she a masochist? Most of her colleagues she'd graduated alongside had long left the profession for something more peaceful. Not that London needed more yoga instructors. Mia had encouraged her to start meditating to help manage the stress. She liked her teacher, Alice, a lot. There was something reassuring about how healthy she looked. The quiet was nice too, but it didn't stop her mind playing an endless loop of scenes from school. Most of the students treated her as they did their beloved technology: something to be played with, an extension of their egos, a way to express outrage at the world. She'd been a sounding board for too long and now she walked around in a fog of suppressed questions.

What makes you afraid of your mother?

Why are you hungover again?

What do you see in your dealer boyfriend?

Why don't you care? Why don't you care? Why don't you care?

Before he was assigned to her, Bettie had seen Daniel when she was on duty in the poolroom. He'd yell 'Check out my new polo shirt' with the same ferocity as 'I'm not fuckin' playing you again – you cheatin' cocksucker!' But beneath his bravado, Daniel was a kind boy, and patient.

He helped the younger kids move the tables aside in the hall for drama practice, knew how to talk to the students with learning needs. He'd been in trouble with the police a few times because he wanted things and didn't seem to mind who they belonged to. But she couldn't blame him for that desire really. It was a rare human who didn't go through life coveting what other people thrust in their face. He just had to learn how to handle it better.

'Open up, Bettie!' Tiny fists pummelled on the win-dowed door. Tracey: fifteen years old and the energy of a full brass band. Her pink hair was wound into two buns on either side of her head in an uncanny replica of Daniel's snack. Tracey had been on after-school tuition for weeks – excluded for spitting at the other students. She teetered between girlhood and womanhood but hadn't yet plunged into it like the other girls her age – bragging about sex, wanting everyone to know who they're having it with, and in what position. There was something elegant about her when she flew into a rage. Perhaps it was the purity of it – everything imbued with urgency. Bettie missed that, in a way.

'Lemme in,' Tracey shouted through the glass. She turned in a circle, stopped, took a breath and hit the door harder, screwing up her face so that she looked both six and sixty years old.

The magnetic doors made Bettie uncomfortable. They stopped the kids bursting in and out of the classrooms but

kept them physically and metaphorically on the outside –
something they'd already experienced too often.

'Shut the fuck up, man,' Daniel yelled.

'Fuck off, prick.'

'Tracey, you've gotta think more about how you speak
to people when you want them to do something for you,'
Bettie said, holding her ID card to the magnetic strip and
opening the door.

Tracey cleared her throat. 'Bettie, I'm so terribly sorry
to interrupt your class. I left my animals in there.' She
pointed at the stack of exercise books. 'I need them for
textiles. Now.'

'I've asked you not to sew in my lessons.' Bettie walked
over to the bookcase and retrieved Tracey's English exercise book. Tucked inside was a piece of red felt with cat
and dog faces made with hair Tracey collected from her
cat. Apparently it was an art form.

'Ta,' she said, dashing back out through the door
and into the classroom opposite. Bettie stared at the
empty corridor, the white paint scuffed where the kids
had kicked the walls earlier that day. In preparation for
parents' evening, the deputy head spent yesterday on her
hands and knees with a Magic Eraser sponge, scrubbing
at the marks.

'It's not fair that the girls get to do textiles,' Daniel said.

'There's no rule about that? You could take the class if
you wanted to. *Do* you want to?'

'I don't have time to have the shit ripped out of me.'

He leaned back in his chair, looking as if he were going to say something further but then thinking better of it. He scrunched his nose, scratched his head and cleared his throat. Daniel always seemed to be hovering on the edge of a confession. She waited, hoping that he'd come out with it. But he just studied the exam paper as if the answers were hidden in there somewhere.

She eyed the clock hanging on a rusted nail above the door.

'Bettie, what's that word again? The one where it's like when a word makes you think of other random things?'

'Connotation?'

'Yeah!'

'I remember you telling me that was a useless word.'

'Well when am I gonna use it in real life? But red's used a lot in this article. And we talked about that colour, right? Like how it makes you think of anger, or danger?'

'We did. Well remembered. And love too. Red makes us think about love. Red hearts, roses. All that awful stuff.' She raised an eyebrow.

'I think love is more like the colour yellow, though.'

'You do?'

'Yeah. Like, when you love something, really love it, you get a feeling – a yellow feeling, like the sun, you know?'

'That's lovely.'

He sniffed. 'How come you don't wear a wedding ring?'

'Don't push it.'

He bent his head to write again. Maybe he did have a chance after all. She tried to think of what colour loving Mia felt like. Daniel was right – nothing like red hearts or roses came to mind. It was too abstract for that. A warmth more than anything else. The way she adored the birthmark that straddled Mia's bottom lip and chin. Bettie wound her hair around a finger and a grey caught the light. She plucked it out and wondered if Daniel could sense how she wanted to get out of here as much as he did, counting down the minutes until the lesson ended.

She looked at his paper. He'd attempted more questions than she'd expected. 'OK, it's quarter to five. You're free. I'll see you next week.'

'Thank fuck.'

Daniel scooped up his belongings, stuffed them into his rucksack and burst out of the classroom's back door – the way he knew he wasn't supposed to go. Outside, a few girls lingered at the school gate, smoking and passing around make-up wipes as they slipped back into their hijabs before the walk home.

She stood by the window and watched him for a moment. There was no playground, just a small court-yard which was an eighties horror of red brick and green plastic. Barbed wire stretched along the high walls. Daniel leaned against the ping-pong table. It had lost a leg last year and no one had bothered to take it away. He took out rolling papers and tobacco, and as he made the cigarette he had the deepest look of concentration she'd seen all afternoon. He settled a baseball cap low on his brow before lighting his smoke. Flags of the students' countries of origin flapped above his head.

Where would Daniel end up after school? She imagined him at summer prom. For all the lip he gave, she knew he'd probably skulk around the edges of the dance floor, wearing his cap low over his eyes. Gorge himself on Haribo, drink too many cans of Rio, then mouth off to the girls grinding against the other boys. More likely, he wouldn't turn up. But beyond that – she hadn't a clue. Would he be a stay-at-home dad? Would he end up in jail? Graduate with an honours degree? Work the Tesco checkout until he retired? Maybe found a successful fashion company, wind up a millionaire? So many possible avenues awaited Daniel but she'd never get to know which one would claim him.

He swaggered through the iron gates and on to the main road, headed home, to his girlfriend's, or to work. She closed the back door, turned the key in the lock, and lowered the blinds. If she hurried, she could make another coffee before the afternoon meeting. She gathered her lesson planner and register and saw that Daniel had left a pile of pastry crumbs on the table.

*

'No standing on the upper decks or stairs please,' the electronic voice repeated.

Bettie was at the back of the bus, a place she usually avoided because it was the kids' spot, but today she didn't have a choice. She was thankful to have even made it on – the last one had been too full to stop. She swayed a little and worried she might fall, but the round bellies of strangers held her up. If they shifted even slightly she'd topple – the pole out of reach, her huge handbag resting on her feet. Sweat crept down her neck, between her breasts and into the small of her back. Damp patches grew across the shirts of everyone around her, like ink tipped into water. The opening and closing of the door provided little relief, just a pneumatic hiss.

More people piled in, elbows first. A couple pushed their way out. A boy, eleven or twelve years old, stood by the buggies and refused the space next to his mum. Bettie caught her eye. 'He's a big man, now,' she mouthed. They laughed, but then Bettie began to think again about what would happen if Mia had a boy? So much responsibility, to raise a man right. With girls it was easier – you taught them to guard their bodies, to stay safe, grow up and out and be limitless. But boys – well you had to teach them how to treat girls, how to treat women. He'd have no immediate father figure. How would they talk to him about puberty, about sex? The male body was a mystery to her.

Through the window, she could see the remains of a Stout and Ale sign etched into the brickwork of what was now a cash and carry. The graffiti sprayed across the sides of shops looked like the bubble writing the girls loved to doodle on the front of their exercise books, except instead of *Tina and Jay Forever*, it was *Do We Need Another Tesco Metro?* and *Shit House to Penthouse.*

The CCTV screen was broken, projecting a loop of flickering grey dots where the live images of passengers should be. She thought she heard Daniel's voice but the teenagers storming down the stairs were wearing the uniform of the private school nearby, the school Mia thought Bettie should try and get a job at if they became pregnant. She could nearly double her salary, have even longer breaks between terms. Less risk of being spat at in the eye. What Mia didn't realize was that the rich kids came with a similar set of problems. Entitlement, yes, and that could be a bore. Access to money made for bigger drug problems. But also the same kind of neglect her lot at the PRU experienced.

The bus fell silent, full of quiet, worn-down bodies, headphones in, staring into their phones, giving themselves up to the stifling crush of the journey. Her stomach rumbled.

Six more stops. Ten minutes until she got home to Mia. Fourteen hours until work again.

Outside, London had embraced spring by rolling up its shirtsleeves and drinking earlier than usual. There were suddenly so many more people visible, like the population had swollen in the unexpected heat. Skin pinked as they clustered outside restaurants and bars, blocking the pavements, sitting on the kerb. Aperol Spritz. San Miguel. It seemed like a new cocktail bar or restaurant opened every week. The city had dressed up like Europe again and everyone was saying how nice London is when the sun's out. Cranes on building sites cast a dappled shade and for a moment Hackney looked beautiful.

The road was packed with cars, windows wound down, music blasting, drivers squinting into the sun. Bettie walked down Mare Street through a cloud of cherry-flavoured vape smoke. Towards the park, the twenty-somethings got louder and louder as they worked on tomorrow's hangovers. She caught snippets of their conversation – comparisons of phone cameras, casual mentions of the latest terror attack, who slept with who at the office.

There was a police van by the side of the road, and she caught the eye of a young man they were arresting. She was chilled by the look on his face – either surprised at how his life was about to change irreparably, or else a confirmation of something he already knew. He looked like someone she used to teach before she met Mia, a young man who'd gone down for arson during the London riots. He'd been a sweet kid, so polite.

They'd lived on opposite sides of the city for years before Bettie finally agreed to move in with Mia. She'd always despised Hackney: south and east London as good as different worlds. The loveliness of their street still startled her. So much green, the way evening sun marbled amber brick. Most of the houses along the park had conservatories that led on to pebbled patios, gardens with washing lines, paddling pools, hydrangeas which always seemed to be in bloom. Being able to name flowers was a new pleasure. It was nothing like the crush and noise of her old place in Brixton.

Over the years, all of the flats she'd lived in felt suspended in time, too busy with perpetual comings and goings to ever settle in the present. Always full of broken, borrowed furniture, the fear of a deposit not returned. She'd yet to think of Mia's split-level flat as theirs. It was stuffed into a cul-de-sac, a new building hidden from the main road, but it had a sense of permanence about it, like it was trying hard to fit in among the Georgian glory. Trying so hard there was also something sleazy about it – cladding the colour of melting butter, greasing its way into the neighbourhood.

What the flat had in location it lacked in size. Kitchen, bedroom, and what was once the living room now catered for the overspill from Mia's studio. The floors and walls were lined with easels and canvases, the sink smeared with watery greens and browns, paintbrushes soaking in a pot of lacquer thinner. The oak table Mia got cheap by flirting with the second-hand furniture dealer in the Bethnal Green arches took up most of the kitchen. The bathroom had a tiny shower full of hanging plants, making it impossible to bend down and shave your legs. Mia did not believe in personal space or boundaries. There were no blinds on the ground floor and she breezed around naked.

Bettie fumbled for the keys in her handbag, trying to wedge her hand beneath the pile of exercise books waiting to be marked. Kids in the street lobbed a half-inflated ball between them. It narrowly missed her head. She shuddered, remembering the classroom globe incident. A young girl with a T-shirt covered in pandas stared at her.

Inside, Mia was listening to Bolero and the music reverberated through the flat. Was it Amalia Mendoza again? Ranchera was her latest obsession. Bettie struggled through the hallway, knocking over a potted plant with her bag. The song was coming from the kitchen. Mia had been making borscht for days now, trying to perfect the balance between beetroot and potato. Once she'd got it into her head to try something new, she wouldn't stop before she'd mastered it. The air was heavy with boiled beetroot – the flat even smelled purple.

She slipped off her brogues and saw Mia's silhouette through the open door. The fitted kitchen was new but already seemed out of date. The small tiles were impossible to keep clean. The gaps between the old floorboards, lovingly sanded smooth again, swallowed dropped food, hairbands and pennies. Mia was straight-backed on a wooden stool, chopping lemons on the breakfast counter, crushing their juice into a bowl. Her slender frame was wrapped in an orange dress latticed with coral beads. Gold drop earrings reached her shoulders and loops of gold charm bracelets wound up her arms. She sang along to the record in some semblance of Spanish – off-key but charming. The violins swelled as she stirred in distracted circles. She seemed lost in pleasant monotony.

The evening was turning pale pink through the window behind Mia, the sun still clinging to the city. A vase of lilacs spilled over the stack of washing-up drying on the side. The whole scene looked so beautiful, Bettie let her be for a moment and slipped upstairs to wash the day from her face.

The taps were old, scavenged from a scrapyard, and creaked as they were turned. The water gushed into the porcelain basin, a blue-grey stream hurtling towards the drain. She dotted jasmine oil on her pulse points, swiped balm across her lips, and sighed at her reflection in the mirror. There was never a day when she didn't look tired.

Downstairs, Mia had set the table for dinner. Heavy, earthy-toned ceramic bowls, wine glasses from the guy on Broadway market. Mia always lit candles. She was still singing: something about having faith before loving.

It would take time before the flat felt like home but Bettie was trying. She took note of where the light fell across the bedroom, when it clung to the corners, how six o'clock in the evening cast the best shadows – the ones Mia liked to paint. She'd figured out which chair was the most comfortable to do her marking in, where to step at night to avoid the floorboard that creaked outside the bathroom.

Four years together. One year living here. With a little luck, many more to come. She wanted it to only be the two of them, always. But she'd put Mia's needs before her own. Wasn't that what you were supposed to do for the one you love?

Bettie walked over to the stove, curled an arm around Mia's shoulders and lifted the long dark hair from the nape of her neck, kissing the exposed flesh. It goose-bumped. She smelled of verbena. Mia took her hand and let her fingers play in the palms. She turned down the music.

'How was school? Isn't it hot?'

'It was another day. Wine in the fridge? Did you get the portrait finished?'

'Yes, nice and cold but none for me. You know what, I did, and the brat even thanked me.'

Bettie slid the sharp point of the corkscrew around the seal, twisting the bottle in her hand. It was cool and solid. 'What does it feel like to be thanked?'

Mia laughed. 'I was so shocked I forgot to say you're welcome.' Still stirring, she tilted her head so that Bettie could brush her mouth against the birthmark on the side of her chin, and kiss her plump bottom lip, pulling it gently with her teeth. The song stopped. The silence was wonderful.

'Borscht again?'

'Last time. I promise. I've almost got it.'

Mia's fingers stroked the side of Bettie's ribs, travelling down into the dip of her waist, pulling her closer. Pleasure rippled through her. Waves of it. Not yellow: blue. Love was sky-blue. Like looking out of an aeroplane window for the first time.

May

Two Smokers

Freddy knew his birthday party was really an excuse for his dad to invite the whole family over. He was drowning in conversation that went like this: food, gossip, health, freak weather, regular weather, gossip, food. All he wanted was quiet – that, and a bit of cash for new clothes. But the flat was overflowing with people and, even up on the rooftop, the fresh air had been hijacked by girly perfume, blue cheese and baby vomit. At least it meant everyone was too busy to notice that his best friend Patrick hadn't turned up.

He endured a series of handshakes, wet lipstick kisses and hearty slaps on the back till one nearly knocked him off his feet.

'Happy birthday, kiddo!' Uncle Angelo said. 'Sixteen, eh. The first year of real fun.' Uncle Angelo was trying not to look at his fat lip. His dad must've asked everyone not to bring it up.

Even though they were a similar height, Uncle Angelo leaned down, grabbed his face, and kissed both cheeks. The force of it backed him further into the corner of the roof. He produced a white envelope with *Freddy Boy* scrawled across it. It felt lighter than the one he got on his thirteenth birthday but heavier than it did the last two years.

'Thanks, Uncle A,' he said. 'I'm saving for new clothes.'

'Gotta look nice for the girls.' He winked.

Freddy put on a smile. It hurt his lip. He was thankful for the sambuca he'd sneaked from the fridge before everyone arrived. The pads of his fingers were still sticky from the bottle.

'Got yourself a girlfriend yet?' Uncle Angelo asked. 'They must love how tall you are, right? That's always been my winning card – that, and having loads of cash.' He boomed his banker's laugh.

Uncle Angelo was loaded and Freddy's dad was handsome – that was how it worked.

Freddy checked his phone. Nothing.

'Where's your sister?'

Lyddie was always hiding. They found her in the weirdest places. Underneath the rocking chair in the front room, the car boot, in the tumble dryer with his dog Rupert. Today he thought Lyddie might be on to something. 'No idea,' he replied.

Uncle Angelo wiped his brow with the monogrammed

handkerchief he kept in the pocket of his linen jacket. Freddy wished the weather would chill out; it was far too hot for May. His shirt was suffocating, the trousers Monty had made him stuck to his legs. He shifted the crotch; smoothed the cotton over his knees. He hated this outfit, only wore it to please his mum, who only wanted to please Uncle Wolfie. Monty's death had been sudden. Uncle Wolfie hadn't taken it well.

He surveyed the scene. His mum had arranged umbrellas by the deckchairs to stop guests from overheating. To anyone who'd listen she said, 'Of course it's nothing like home, this heat. It's nothing like home.' She loved to talk about the weather – it was the first British thing she'd learned to do when they came over from Veneto. The whole family were the colour of tree trunks all year round, especially Uncle Angelo, who kept his skin oiled and soaked red-brown. He had two impressive frown lines that stretched across his forehead like McDonald's golden arches. Freddy couldn't look at him without wanting a Big Mac. He probably had a good body once but now the muscle had run to fat, which was why he was shaking his head at the burrata thrust under his nose. 'You know I got a personal trainer to help lose this gut, Luca,' he said, patting his belly. 'Cruel to tempt me with cheese.'

Freddy reckoned his new healthy attitude had a lot to do with his new wife, Inga. He met her on a business trip to Moscow. She was only twenty-three and her lips were always heavy with pink gloss and they stuck together with a smacking sound when she talked like she'd just eaten something delicious. Inga spotted him staring at her and smiled. Her dress seemed to be strips of bandages sewn together and it was so clean and so white, it looked boiled. He tried not to look at her fake boobs.

'Happy birthday!' she said. 'You are real man now. No more baby boy.' She lit a cigarette from the tip of her last one and dropped the sticky butt on to the roof, killing it with the heel of her stiletto. His mum dashed over and slipped an ashtray in front of her. It had a beach scene glazed on it and BENIDORM in coral around the rim. Inga gave her a languid look. 'Grazie mille, Elena,' she said, exhaling a plume of smoke. Freddy wished he could spark up with her.

A blue triangle broke away from the bunting and was carried by the breeze. They'd used the same decorations for Lyddie's tenth birthday and Easter Sunday. He followed its flight down to Uncle Wolfie's freshly mown lawn and then across the street. The pavement was too clean because his mum had swept away sandwich cartons and fag butts that morning. Four discarded Marlboro Lights belonged to him, but so far he'd managed to keep his smoking secret. His dad lived by a lot of trite sayings he read on a daily inspirational quote app, and one of his favourites was *Secrets Will Kill You*, but Freddy reckoned the fags would get there first. And, unlike his dad, he also happened to know his mum smoked. All nurses did – he guessed it was the stress.

Five Things About His Parents

1. There used to be a kick-thump sound from their bedroom. He worked out what it was when he was younger and it grossed him out, but now there's only silence.

2. When the back door banged really hard, he knew his dad was on his way over to Uncle Wolfie's.

3. When his dad left, his mum headed for Lyddie's room. When he wasn't home, Freddy could tell they'd had a fight because Lyddie's hair was French-braided.

4. After they'd finished shouting, his mum cleaned and his dad cooked and everything swung back to normal – except the house had a creepy silence to it like when you're sick and home from school.

5. No matter what, his mum always smelled like stewed apples and cinnamon. He'd no idea how – she never cooked.

At least Freddy had the park to escape to. When he was younger, he'd bike around there with Patrick, or try to BMX. Now, they met on the roof, and on nights when he needed a smoke, he'd wait till everyone was asleep and creep up the stairs to the fire escape. The ladder was long and thin, with even thinner wooden rungs. They'd been painted white, and he was forever picking flecks from his clothes.

From there he could see across the park, and the street beyond it, and it was like a theatre where he was the only one in the audience. He'd get high, look at the stars, imagine what it would be like to be light years away. Patrick biked over on nights when his mum managed the fancy tapas place in town. They'd been best mates since Reception when he dared Freddy to lift up girls' skirts on the playground and showed him how to spit over the wall into his neighbour's pond. Since then, they did all the same things – played for the football team, wore button-down Fred Perry shirts, smoked Marlboro Lights and listened to the same bands. He'd forgotten if he actually liked any of these things.

Patrick had a lot of hobbies, most of which were about impressing girls. His latest was learning to play the guitar and he'd been composing a song for Ana for the past two weeks. She was the only one in their group who hadn't fallen for his lines. It drove Patrick crazy. He was the captain of the football team, which meant girls usually tripped over themselves when he smiled. But Freddy knew Ana was going to hate the song because a) she liked punk, not the soft indie shit Patrick preferred, and b) she hated attention.

Ana was different. She didn't talk in code like Karly and Tamaya and the other girls at school. In class, she was quiet, did the bare minimum, and then somehow smashed the exams. The whole group knew that Ana's flat was tiny, sandwiched between a Turkish restaurant and a snooker hall, but he was the only one to know that her mum lived here illegally. Even though she'd been with Ana's dad for twenty years, they weren't married and she didn't have papers to stay. She made money running a cleaning company staffed by other illegal Colombians. What he still didn't know was how Ana felt about any of this.

Patrick tried to teach him the guitar, but the only chords he could get his head around were 'Smoke on the Water'.

Last week, while he focused on making smoke rings, Patrick played a few chords of Ana's song and said, 'Good, right? She's gonna like it?'

Freddy decided to tell him the truth. 'Ana's not gonna fall for cheesy lyrics. She's not some fashion punk like Karly. Just be straight up with her.'

Patrick thumped him in the chest and said, 'All right, wanker. Soon as you get laid I'll think about taking your girl advice.'

His mum zipped around the guests like a hummingbird, doling out compliments. She dropped kisses on cheeks, poured more wine, wiped tomato sauce from the kids' faces. All of them looked alike – thin, knobby joints, Mediterranean fuzz, so many he couldn't remember their names. He felt bad knowing that the girls would have to bleach their moustaches when they grew up. One of the boys was on the edge of the decking, swinging his feet. When he thought no one was looking, he gobbed off the side and a little of it caught on his chin, goopy and translucent. He motioned for Freddy to join him but he shook his head. Instead, he stood next to his older cousins who'd formed a line by the speakers propping up the window.

'Fuck sake, when is this gonna be over?' one of them muttered. With crossed arms, they looked past everyone, and said nothing to him. He was grateful.

The buzzer to the block rang and rang and someone was forever running down the fire escape to answer it. His mum was still too spooked to leave the front door open, even though it was ages ago that kid in the park had acid thrown in his face. It was unlike his mum to react like that – as a nurse she'd seen it all. But he guessed the boy had been too close his own age for her to ignore. They'd seen reports of it on the news again now that he'd woken up from his coma. No one had been arrested yet.

He checked his phone. Nothing.

'There he is! The man of the hour.' This was Aunt Bea, Uncle Angelo's first wife. She kissed him and pressed a white envelope into his hands. It was seriously bulky.

'Thank you!' he said, trying to guess the amount inside.

She took a step back and looked at him, her eyes lingering for a moment on his fat lip. 'How did you get to be such a grown man? Sixteen!'

He shrugged.

'I remember the day you were born – long legs, even then. Did you win your last match? Got a girlfriend yet?'

He blushed. 'Thanks for the cash. I'm saving for new clothes.'

'My pleasure, sweet pea.' She grabbed his mum's arm as she passed with a bottle of wine. 'Elena. Slow down. Enjoy yourself. Where's Lydia? How's her painting coming along?'

'So good. A natural artistic eye.'

'Must've got it from her mother,' Aunt Bea said.

His dad came and kissed Aunt Bea on the cheek. 'Lyddie mostly draws pandas. I sort of wish she'd expand her oeuvre.'

His mum's head snapped up. 'It's important we just encourage her art.' She paused then took Aunt Bea's glass and the bottle glugged as she poured. 'More wine?'

'That colour looks good on you, Bea,' his dad said.

'It was Elena's dress, actually. She gave it to me.' She lowered her voice to a whisper. 'Have you seen someone's brought gluten-free lasagne with them?'

Freddy tuned out. On the street below, a man in a tracksuit walked by, yelling into his phone. A BMW flashed past, then an ambulance. Two of his neighbours were yelling at each other because they wanted the parking space away from the tree to avoid the bird shit. He didn't know why they weren't more concerned about the environment. The planet was set to implode, they didn't need to drive at all. Monty left Uncle Wolfie his battered green Astra when he died but Wolfie had sold it for scrap – he knew no one needed a car in London. It was odd, Monty not being here today. Even if he hated these trousers, he'd always admired Monty's brightly coloured suits, the way he put outfits together. The funeral was colourful too, nothing like he'd expected, and it was full of people he'd never seen before. He leaned out over the edge of the roof. On the opposite side of the street, just within sight, was Monty's house, shrouded in scaffolding. It sold super-fast to some woman named Caroline that Wolfie couldn't stand. Parts of the building had already been pulled down and put back again in a different configuration. There was always a heap of bricks in the drive. Beyond the park's gate, the grass was dry from the heatwave. He tried to imagine all the things that might be happening over there at the same time as things were happening at the party. A shoot bursting through the soil, a flower unfurling, a line of ants carrying a piece of apple. It would be nice to curl up in the grass. Read a book. All that would bother him would be the bugs and at least they couldn't ask him questions.

*

Aunt Mona was by the food table, slapping at the air, shooing a swarm of wasps. They buzzed away, then back, hovering motionless over the food, daring her to try again. Her blue skirt swished with each swat and she made little *hah hah* sounds. Mona was his favourite aunt, even though she wasn't technically family, because she was the toughest person he knew, even tougher than Ana. He didn't know what to do about her being sick, so he helped her in the garden on Saturday mornings before football practice. She told him how over the years she'd worked the soil with bonemeal and compost, turning its chalky texture into a sandy loam. He trowelled the top layer, which was soft and crumbly with a rich sour smell, his thumbs pressing the oniony skin of bulbs into the damp. It was good to try something new every year, she said, and bought her plants from Pete's stall on Columbia Road. He learned to recognize narcissus, iris, hyacinth, dahlias, begonias. Mona loved yellow, and the shades reminded him of his dad's cooking: buttermilk, lemon meringue, egg yolks. He hoped that Uncle Wolfie would let her stay in their house long enough to see them grow. He couldn't bear the idea of Aunt Mona in a care home.

Aunt Mona squinted up at him. 'How the hell did you get that fat lip?'

He felt the red prickle across his neck. 'Footy practice.'

'Likely story,' she said. 'You need to look after that handsome punim. Help me arrange these dishes. Too many things on this table.'

Everyone was told to bring their signature dish but, as always, they arrived with two. Plates were mountainous with pizzettas, salami, prosciutto, a whole smoked salmon, cheeses, rice salad, potato salad, Caprese salad, sotto aceti, bruschetta, and aubergine parmigiana. He was mortified – there was no way it would all get eaten. He knew it took six years just to break down a head of lettuce in a landfill.

'I don't know who these people are,' Aunt Mona said, waving a hand around. 'It's horrible here.'

'Agreed.' He smiled, relieved she was having one of her better days.

'Have you seen the fridge? It's stacked with sweet things. Someone will have to bring out another table just for the puddings. Gluttons.'

She stopped fussing with the food and took a long look at him. 'What awful trousers. You're far too tall and too thin for them. They belong in the bin, darling.'

He laughed.

The shock of Uncle Wolfie's white hair arrived first as he slowly climbed the fire-escape stairs on to the roof. He put one arm around Aunt Mona and extended his other hand to Freddy. It felt dry and heavy.

'Happy birthday, Federico, my boy,' he said. 'You have all the best years to come.' He kissed his cheeks, slipped his hand into the pocket of his blazer and handed him a white envelope.

'Thank you.' He put it on the table next to the others. 'I'm saving for new clothes.'

'Let's toast you, Freddy,' Uncle Wolfie said, pouring a glass of red from an open bottle.

He didn't like the bitter taste of wine, but accepted the drink to top up the shots of sambuca. Parties were always better when they were a bit swimmy.

The last time he got really drunk was with Ana at Patrick's place. Tamaya and Karly were upstairs dyeing each other's hair black and Patrick and Rashid had cycled to the petrol station to buy fags. Ana pulled out a bottle of aguardiente she'd swiped from home – some local stuff her aunt brought over from Bogotá.

'It tastes like liquorice,' she said. As she tipped the bottle back, he watched her throat move when she swallowed. There was a silver skull on her necklace. Its eyes sparkled. Her skin was so white it seemed tinged with blue – it matched the streaks in her dark hair, and the battered blue Doc Martens he'd never seen her take off. She exhaled loudly, whistled, and then grinned – a single crooked tooth in a row of straight white ones.

'Here,' she said. 'It's good shit.'

He swigged and felt fire. It was nothing like the liquorice he and Lyddie bought at the corner shop. He coughed and she laughed. When he handed the bottle back, she farted loudly and laughed some more. Nothing embarrassed her. Patrick had heard that Ana and her two sisters shared a bedroom but he might have made that up. She never talked about home.

Ana might be the only person he knew who was *real*.

She passed him the booze again. 'Why is Patrick such a dick to me all the time?'

'He is?'

She tipped the ash from her fag into a plant pot. 'Yeah. He always says the opposite to what I say. To spite me or something.'

'I dunno about that.'

'You're so different from him.' She took a long draw from the bottle. 'How did you end up so close? He thinks he's some alternative guy, with his guitar and that, but he's more like a jock.'

'He's my best friend,' he said, shrugging, and that's when she leaned across the sofa, smoothed his hair down and put the end of her cigarette in his mouth.

He checked his phone. Nothing.

Across the roof, his dad and Uncle Angelo stood shoulder to shoulder, squinting into the distance. His dad ran his hands through his black curls – he loved to draw attention to them. Uncle Angelo was balding at the crown. The two of them had a weird relationship. His dad was hung-up because his brother lived in a massive house in Holland Park, so to compensate he liked to talk about how Victoria Park was *affluent*. He also liked to rattle on about how life was difficult for him growing up on the farm after Angelo left for London. But it sounded kind of idyllic to Freddy.

'How was Monty's stone setting yesterday?' Uncle Angelo asked Uncle Wolfie. 'Did you speak to my head-stone guy in the end?' He didn't wait for an answer, but instead launched into a long story about the one time he met Monty. Usually when Uncle Angelo took the floor, Uncle Wolfie would have an expression like he was holding his breath. He couldn't bear it when someone out-storied him. But today he let him talk and talk and he wasn't even drinking his red wine.

The story finally finished. There was silence for a moment, then Uncle Wolfie said, 'People say that you die twice, isn't that so? Once when you pass and then again when everyone who loved you dies.' He stopped, mas-saged the soft dough of his cheek. 'I think the worst thing is that Monty will have two deaths in quick succession.'

Last Saturday, the whole group hung out at Patrick's place after footy practice and played the drinking game Never Have I Ever. Patrick's mum worked weekends, like

Freddy's parents, but he was lucky enough not to have a kid sister hanging around asking a thousand dumb questions a minute, like *Do starfish have faces?* or *What is a Spice Girl?* The flat was pretty tiny but the living room had a fifty-two-inch screen they could watch movies on – which is what usually happened because everyone fought too much about what music to play.

In the garden was a Second World War bunker Patrick had kitted out with beanbags and gangster movie posters. They used it as somewhere to smoke, turning it into a hotbox which, when he thought about it, made him feel a little bad. The bunker quickly filled up with smoke, casting everyone in a pale haze.

'Never have I ever been caught wanking,' Karly said.

All the boys laughed and took a shot.

'That's lame,' Patrick said. 'Of course we've been caught wanking, man. I see the girls are sneakier than us. Well that figures.'

Something had been up with Patrick all night. The game had been going on for ages and everyone was pretty drunk because Patrick was making everyone take a shot of Buckfast instead of chugging beer. It gave Freddy sugar giggles.

They were deep into the game when Patrick blurted out, 'I have never ever shagged Ana.'

Ana yelled, 'Hey arsehole, that's not cool.'

The room went really quiet. Freddy felt his face flame

and stared at his shot. Patrick opened the door. The smoke poured out and he was gone.

Five Things Patrick Said

1. I never knew you were such a pussy hound, you prick.

2. You went bright red. Everyone knows when you're lying.

3. You knew I liked her. How could you do that?

4. How long you been fucking hiding this?

5. Did she blow you?

Everyone crowded around the table, heaping plastic plates with food. Aunt Mona was sitting on her knees whispering to Lyddie, who was hiding underneath. There was food on faces, black specks on teeth. Freddy tuned into the inane chatter.

'Oh God, is that Cece's coleslaw? Why the hell does she put peanuts in it? I mean, peanuts!'

'How did I get sauce on my ear?'

'Actually it's on your nose as well.'

'Yes, they're old and ill. But what can I do? I have three kids, four if you count Tim, and I'm working full time. We barely have enough as it is.'

'Who's that in the house opposite, staring at us through the window?'

'It's that yenta Rose. She's always sitting there. It's so creepy.'

'She's probably lonely.'

'Maybe we should have invited her.'

His dad dug him in the ribs. 'See them out there?' he said, pointing down at the street where Uncle Angelo was shaking his hands at his wife. 'Twenty minutes that's been going on.'

'Guess the honeymoon is over then.'

'Women are tricky, right?'

'Shut up, Dad.'

'Just saying, you could spend a lifetime trying to figure them out. It's important to keep your friends around.'

'That from your inspirational quote app?'

'Shh, you.'

'Hey, where's Joe today?'

'He's coming later. Said he had work to do.'

'More like a girl to kick out of bed.'

'I should tell you off for that but you're probably right.'

From the street he heard, 'Why do you treat me like an idiot all the time?'

'Bychit. You act like idiot, I treat like idiot.'

'You really are a bitch.'

'Go fuck yourself, khuyesos.'

His dad laughed. 'Let's learn how to swear in Russian,' he said. 'Sounds so much better.'

He checked his phone. Nothing.

Five Things He Didn't Tell Patrick

1. Ana's eyes are hazel and he kept whispering, *Nuts, your eyes are like nuts*, in her ear and she kept telling him to shut up.

2. The backseat of her sister's car was littered with empty Heineken cans, Quavers packets and three bottles of Lambrini – one nearly went up his arse and Ana weed herself a bit laughing.

3. Her dress was green, shimmering. Tight at the top and then flowing down over her hips. It caught the light when she moved.

4. The shape her mouth made when he put his hands down her pants.

5. How no one prepares you for how the wetness feels.

'You know, Wolfie tried to propose to me with some fakakta thing he claims was an heirloom,' Aunt Mona was saying. 'But people like us, like Wolfie and me, we don't have heirlooms. So I sent him down to that place in town and I said to him, I said, *Get rid of this and come back with something proper.*'

'Ay-yay-yay!' Uncle Wolfie said. 'And I did. A beautiful deco ring. And now Mona is a proper balabusta.'

'What does that one mean?' Freddy asked. Yiddish impressed Ana more than Italian.

'A good homemaker, a good wife.' Uncle Wolfie touched Mona's arm. 'I think we better take the salmon in. It's going to cook in this sun. Where's your sister gone now? She was here a minute ago! She needs to eat.'

'Sister?' Aunt Mona said. 'What are you talking about?'

Uncle Wolfie caught his eye and slowly shook his head.

'Come on, Aunt Mona,' Freddy said. 'Let's get you some grub.' When he touched her arm it felt like a twig.

Afterwards, Freddy went downstairs to find Lyddie. He caught sight of his mum through the crack in the bath-room door. There was an intense look on her face as she brushed her hair, twisting and turning, trying to find an angle where she liked the way she looked. She chopped it into a bob last month. He thought she looked more glam-orous, but she hated it. She applied more red to her lips, following the curve of her wrist as she followed the curve of her mouth. How did she keep it between the lines?

He heard strange sounds coming from Lyddie's room. She was the favourite, the sweet arty child, which was why her room was so much bigger than his. It was painted black and white and covered with her drawings, which were sort of surreal portraits of pandas and good in a way he couldn't quite explain. Her bedcovers had pandas on them and so did her cushions. The room shone grey from the two white lights under black lampshades. On the windowsill were neat rows of things she liked to hoard. Shells from Brighton beach, apricot kernels, feathers, empty bubblegum wrappers. She arranged then rearranged them.

Lyddie's feet poked out from under her bed. She was making the little clicking noises she used to talk to his dog Rupert. He mewled back at her like a cat. It was a constant disappointment to him that the dog was so dumb.

'What's wrong?' he asked. 'Why are you under there?'

'Everyone keeps pinching my cheeks.'

Lyddie stuck her head out from under the bed. She pushed her fringe out of her eyes. She was the spitting image of their mum; he, on the other hand, looked like his dad – tall and goofy. Everything about her was childlike. Big eyes, shiny blonde hair, the freckles she hated all over her legs and arms. It felt impossible that one day she'd become an adult.

'I did you a painting,' she said. 'Do you want it now or on the real real birthday?'

'Now.'

She handed him a scroll tied with purple ribbon.

'This looks pretty, Lyddie,' he said.

'Open it.'

The ribbon puddled to the floor. He unfurled the paper carefully and felt his body turn to water. The drawing was crude, kind of abstract with intense splodges of colour, but it was clearly of him – there was no denying it – in one of their mum's dresses. The long black one with a slit up one side which she used to wear to weddings.

His heartbeat quickened the way he imagined drowning might feel. And there was a vibrating inside of him, a low throbbing hum. How hadn't he realized before that blood had a *sound*?

'Lyddie!' he said, because he didn't know what else to say. He was sure there was red bruising his neck, spreading to his cheeks.

'Remember what Dad always says? About how secrets will kill you? I don't want you to die, so now you know it's not a secret.'

He couldn't believe she knew. He'd been so careful. A master of caution, in fact. A dam of adrenaline burst inside him like he was hurtling towards something even as he was standing still.

'When?' he managed to ask. 'When did you see?'

'Loads of times, dummy. Hey, do you know what I was wondering?'

'No.'

'When's dessert?'

Five Minutes With Ana

— Why do you keep staring at my dress like that?

— It's nice. The way it shines when the pleats move. You look pretty.

— No guy has ever said anything about my clothes before. Unless it's like, *Take that off.*

— You've been hanging round the wrong guys.

— How do you know they're pleats?

— What?

— No guy knows what a pleat is.

Ana lifted the dress up and over her head. She wasn't wearing a bra and it was the first time he'd seen her naked. Her skin was smooth and pale. Soft. So different from his. He ran his hand across her belly before Ana said:

— Here.

— What you doing?

— Try it.

— Are you high?

— Well, duh. But I won't tell anybody. Trust me.

— What the fuck. Don't be a dick.

— Freddy, it's all right. Just try. It's New Look. Got it last weekend. Take your T-shirt off and slip it on. There you go. You've gotta learn to let go of what you think every-body thinks of you. You can be anything you want to be. You look lovely. Proper lovely. How does it feel?

'Time for cantuccini con vin santo!' his mum said. The sun had thinned out and the clouds had a clothy weight to them, though that could also be from his third glass of wine.

He checked his phone.

Ana, 2:34 p.m.: *How's it going? Roof later?*

Finally.

There was a buzzing in his stomach that he knew wasn't just the drink. It was something deeper and more permanent.

Freddy, 2:34 p.m.: *Torture! Yes, come make it better.*

His mum was slicing the fruit tarts. In a bowl next to her were sugared almonds wrapped in white gauze for guests to take home. She thought of everything. Hands grabbed plates and everyone looked so happy, munching and talking, he considered maybe making more of an effort to talk to people. Get involved. He felt more fluid than usual. He should go and find Lyddie again, put her on his shoulders like she always begged him to do. He caught his mum's eye and smiled, a real warm smile, a thank-you smile, but the one she returned was tight and tense.

He was well aware that, despite Dad's efforts, it was Mum who'd made this party come together. But she looked as trapped as he'd felt all day. And he longed to go to her, to comfort her somehow, put his palm on her forehead the way she had done when he'd broken his arm. But mostly what he wanted was to offer her a cigarette – he could even visualize the packet of twenty Marlboro

Lights, his hand flipping open the top, four fags left, sliding one till it peeked out from the silver foil, nodding his head for her to take it, and her face flaring orange at the spark of his Zippo. If only they could smoke together, then maybe they could be accomplices – not just two people who both turned out to be pretty bad at keeping secrets. But the sound of his dad's laughter from across the roof stopped his hand reaching for the packet.

June

The Dresses

Veronica's plimsolls pummelled down the platform and she made the 8:33 train seconds before the doors beeped and clanged shut. She took a seat, listened to her breath slow. The sweat trickled down her neck and on to the label of her uniform. The carriage was quiet, full of half-asleep bodies, the morning smell of energy drinks and fried bacon sour in the warm air. She exhaled. Dawid had woken her when he left for work at four a.m. and then that was it for sleep. The sheets a sticky pile at the bottom of the bed, her skin clammy. Wide awake, she'd cooked in the heat until it was time to get the girls out of bed, dressed, fed, off to school. And then she'd found the diary.

There were things cleaning women had a sixth sense about and one of them was hiding places. Cigarettes, birth control, belly-button piercings – any rebellion Veronica's daughters tried on for size never stood a chance. So she was stunned, maybe even impressed, when she'd found Ana's diary wedged behind the hallway radiator. She forgot to rescue the fallen sock.

The train was old, the seats poorly upholstered, so when the breeze came through an open window the patterned fabric rose up like puff pastry. The air cooled her burning cheeks. Next to her, a mother adjusted the collar of her daughter's school dress. It was cornflower blue with white lace details, and her straw boater hat had a thick pink ribbon tied around the brim that flopped on to the girl's cheeks as she fidgeted. The woman knocked into Veronica's overstuffed tote bag, which was balanced on her knees. Inside: a change of clothes, a new pack of Marigolds, a tube of coral Revlon lipstick, three tangerines, and Ana's diary. It had been an impulse – to take it with her. She wasn't sure she even wanted an insight into Ana's mind. Finding the birth control had been bad enough. This was what they warned you about: the terrible raw nonsense of raising teenage girls.

The sun shot bright patches of light across the pavement. She passed a few men in grey suits, some in jeans and T-shirts. Women clad in bright cotton dresses and denim jackets, or striding in slacks and blouses, clutched take-away coffee cups that touched the rim of their oversized black sunglasses each time they took a sip. Two of them bit into croissants, another a slice of toast, eating as they

walked and typed and made phone calls, full of caffein-
ated purpose. She could do with another coffee, but her
nerves were jangled enough. She rolled her shoulders,
switched the tote bag to her other arm, and turned into
the park.

Veronica had been cleaning houses around the park
for ten years. Her first client was Monty, a Savile Row
tailor. She had sharp memories of that first afternoon
because she accidentally vacuumed up three sewing
needles which had popped the bag. Dust clumps everywhere! She'd done a good job for him, the street talked;
her number was passed on. No one asked where she
was from, or for a National Insurance number. They
paid cash. Years later, she had a respected cleaning business under Dawid's name, clients appreciated her good
English (though that wasn't something they said out
loud) and her girls were reliable, polite, and knew how
to get a good shine on the stove.

Dogs tore across the grass, desperate in the wake of
orange balls. The path was full of waddling toddlers
in shorts and T-shirts, babies in prams, fat legs kicking
into the air as their parents or nannies stared into the
distance where the swings were waiting to be swung.
She envied the ones with young children who'd not yet
learned to speak or write their thoughts. Boy, did they
have it coming. Ana was quiet and impenetrable. Her
demeanour matched her black hair (that came from

Veronica, the other two had Dawid's blond locks and a much sunnier temperament) and she listened to the kind of punk music Veronica didn't understand the first time round. Sometimes she looked across the dinner table at her daughter shovelling spaghetti into her mouth, scraping blue varnish from her nails, and wondered – where did this being come from?

Rose's flat was the third floor of the corner house. She called out hello and let herself in, quickly rewinding her long dark hair into a neat bun at the top of her head as she walked up the stairs. Rose was the last person she wanted to see. Four cleaners had quit before her so now Rose's daughter paid double the rate for an hour. She could understand why the poor woman threw money, rather than time, at the situation. Rose was a horror. Veronica went through the motions – change of shoes, kettle on, products and broom and mop out from the cupboard – all the while musing how neon-green was an odd colour choice for a diary.

Rose was in an armchair by the window, staring out into the street. She turned her head momentarily, nodded hello.

'Let's get some windows open in here, shall we?' Veronica said. She struggled with the old mechanism to the wide bay until it gave and fresh air rushed into the stuffy room.

Rose tutted. 'What did you do that for? You know how I get cold.' The table next to her was littered with cigarette burns spoiling the walnut grain. When she thought Veronica wasn't looking, she used her good hand to push coasters over the marks. There were no family photographs – all surfaces were covered with ugly china figurines. They collected an unreal amount of dust.

'Careful with those!' Rose called out.

Her Irish accent was pillow-soft. It made her foul mouth all the more sinister. Vodka was supposed to have an undetectable smell, but Veronica knew that drink enough and it gave a mist to a person's breath like the ethanol in cleaning products – milky, a little sweet. Rose was canny, though. It took Veronica a while to discover where she hid the bottles.

'Heaven knows how you became a cleaner with those large clumsy hands of yours.'

She kept dusting and tried not to look a china frog in the eye. There was a pretty spray of flowers next to it that Rose's daughter must have bought.

'I see you, eyeing that. I know your kind. Don't think I won't notice if it magically goes walkies.'

Even as Veronica replied, 'Come now, you know I don't steal,' she could see Ana screaming and shouting as she returned from school and found her diary missing.

'Pull the books off the shelf when you dust it, girl. Honestly, you people are so lazy.'

'You know there's not enough time. We've been through this.'

'Be careful with that, it's a limited edition!'

'Dante's *Inferno*. "In the middle of the journey of our life I found myself within a dark wood where the straight way was lost."'

'Ah, so she can read.'

'I have a degree in European Literature.'

'They teach literature at the university for cleaning ladies, do they?'

Veronica clucked her tongue, returned the book and kept dusting. No use answering back. It was hard to believe Rose was a reader, interested in different worlds, different kinds of people. Sometimes Veronica allowed herself to think about the sugar tang of guarapo, the smell of real heat, or how the three white crosses of El Cerro could fool you into thinking you were already in the next world, but less often now.

She turned to Rose. 'Time for the windows.'

Rose shot her an icy look, her face gullied with lines. She was beautiful once, you could tell, might still be if she wasn't frowning all the time. Veronica bent down, supported Rose by the elbow, and helped her across the room. She felt lighter every week.

The ugly paisley sofa creaked in protest as Rose sank into its folds, the coils old and resisting. But at least it was being used. Veronica mistrusted furniture that looked as if no one had ever sat in it. The best couches were a little worn, those where you could see a backside had been thankful for the cushion.

She sprayed the window where Rose's breath had made white clouds and then towelled it off in a series of circles. The vinegar tang helped mask the sulphur scent of old age. People didn't know how their own homes smelled. Not cooking odours or perfume, though those could linger as well. No, some houses smelled like melting plastic, or the bitter green of a split sapling. Others like an old candyfloss stick. It didn't matter how strong the products she used were, or how powerful the vacuum, she couldn't suck their smells from the corners.

'You finished yet?' Rose asked.

She kept polishing, shine replacing smears.

'Do you hear me?'

'Loud and clear.'

'Heaven above, you're slow.'

As she returned a glaring Rose to the armchair, she knew she'd have to make it home before Ana that evening. She couldn't bear it if her daughter were to look at her the way Rose did, like she was an intruder in her world.

'You've bleach on that uniform of yours, girl.'

She looked down and saw the off-white stain. How could she have missed that this morning? She shrugged. 'Occupational hazard.'

'It's slobbish. What's the point in dressing smart if it's covered in muck?'

'That's enough, now.'

Rose fell silent and turned back to the window. That was all she wanted, really – to push and push and be told when she'd reached the limit, where the boundary lay. But she was right about the bleach stain. It didn't look good. She'd designed the uniforms herself. Duck-egg-blue tunic, Cali Cleaning Company logo in silver, grey cigarette pants. They were smart, more like a beautician's uniform. This way, clients felt they were getting a specialist service, like having a carpet deep-cleaned, or the house fumigated – anything to mask the feeling they'd hired a servant.

You can go straight to a person's core by finding out how they treat their cleaning lady. Any service industry staff, really. She'd dumped a couple of handsome men in her time after they'd disrespected their waitress with a terse comment. She laundered all the girls' uniforms herself so she could sniff them before they went into the machine. She needed to check that they were sweat-reeking and soaked with nose-stinging cleaning fluids. It was a little unkind, but it was her reputation, her liveli-hood on the line.

She shut Rose's front door behind her and sat with her handbag on her lap on the stone steps. The outline of the diary dug into her thigh. She hadn't time to eat earlier, so plucked a tangerine from her bag and peeled it slowly. Then she took out the diary. It fell open to a random page. She glanced at it, one eye shut, and then stopped kidding herself.

Sep. 12

Mr Murray actually taught us something interesting today. Almost made me sorry they're getting rid of GCSE music. It was about Shepard tone and the way it's like a spinning barbershop pole, its colours looking like it could go on forever. Ad Infinitum, which I think is a good band name. Shepard tone does the same thing with sound by layering three sine waves, separated by octaves. The middle-octave scale stays at a constant volume, the top one fades out and then the bottom fades in. Then, when it's played on a loop, it tricks our brains into thinking the tone is ascending, growing, building towards something but actually NOTHING'S changed in the music or volume or tone. It's just an illusion. The sound is going nowhere. And I was thinking fuck yes – now I've got proof music is like life! And then Mr Murray told me off for swinging on my chair. Fuck that boring bastard.

Veronica sighed. Apart from the foul language, it was innocent enough. But she couldn't shake her unease, the sense that she'd got lucky. She checked her watch: twenty minutes before she was due at Wolfie and Mona's. Her mami always said everything felt better on a full belly, so she stood and headed to the deli to see Luca. Ana had no idea that she knew her boyfriend's dad. Some things you wanted to keep for yourself. And she had a bit of a crush on Luca – his dark curls, wide smile. How he seemed to have no idea how handsome he was. She dumped the tangerine peel in the bin and pushed open the door of Wolfie's deli. It was empty.

'Ciao, amore mio,' Luca said.

'Ciao, amore.' She settled on the bar stool. Her knees ached and she rubbed her neck, sore from stooping as she hoovered. Jazz played quietly from a tinny speaker wedged between the meat slicer and coffee machine.

Luca reached for a white bagel, sliced it in half, and pushed it into the toaster.

'How was the old bat this morning?' he asked.

'Her usual joyful self.'

Luca opened a tub of Wolfie's egg mayonnaise. She liked to watch Wolfie make mayonnaise when she did his house. He had such a sweet frown of concentration as he cooked, she forgave the mutinous piles of coriander on the parquet floor, fish bones wedged in the tile grout, olive-oil fingerprints on every surface. She found matzo crumbs year-round. He sang sometimes when he cooked. Always Jewish folk songs. They all sounded sad.

'Been busy?' she asked.

He shook his head, twisted the pepper grinder three times and slid the plate across the counter. 'One day you'll quit that racist. Or club her over the head with a vodka bottle. Either would do.'

'That's one mess I wouldn't mind clearing up.' She bit into the bagel. The egg was cool and creamy on the warm sweet bread.

The door shuddered and chimed and a beautiful woman glided in, gold charm bracelets jangling.

'Ciao, Mia,' Luca said. 'Salmon?'

'Four hundred grams, please, lovely.'

'Still going with the pâté project, then?' Luca asked.

She nodded. 'Last batch was too lemony. Bettie has made me promise this is the last lot. She doesn't understand: these hormone injections mess with my taste buds. I get fixated on one food. I can't explain it.'

Veronica smiled up at the woman, who caught her eye and smiled back. Was she trying to get pregnant? Veronica just had to hold hands with Dawid and bam, another girl would pop out nine months later. She'd barely had time to think between pregnancies.

With Luca occupied, she slipped the diary from her bag. She flipped through the pages. So many! Ana had gripped the black biro with such intensity it had left grooves in the paper.

Feb. 11

Skipped afternoon classes and went West End with Freddy. I love shopping with him. I think Karly's getting fed up with me and him being together all the time but if she'd ever been in love she'd totally get it. *Who'd wanna go shopping with you anyway*, she said. *You only ever buy black stuff.* She was wearing all black when she said that, including her fingernails. Hypocrite. Sometimes I think Karly is just <u>young</u>. But even if I wanted her to join us shopping, she couldn't. The best bit is watching Freddy's face light up when we sneak into the changing rooms. He starts off really shy but when he has a dress on he sort of glows from the inside. He looks so beautiful in whatever he wears it's almost unfair. I guess I must be selfish deep down because I love to be the only person who gets to see him when he's like that.

¡Dios mio! She slammed the book shut. Freddy liked to wear dresses? That sweet boy? A pervert? How could Ana stand it? Dawid would hit the roof if he knew his daughter was spending time with a boy like that. These kids were something else, playing dress-up like they were toddlers.

She looked up at Luca, wrapping oily salmon in layers of greaseproof paper. He had such masculine hands. Did he know what his son was up to? She shook her head. There was so much bravado among men. Did it make the relationship between fathers and sons more or less complicated than mothers and daughters?

The woman handed him a crumpled note. There was a blackboard nailed to the wall with the prices in faded chalk that no one consulted. Flecks of blue paint on her fingernails caught the light as she cupped her hand to take the change. 'Ciao,' she said. When she turned to leave, Veronica saw a flash of a violent birthmark across her olive skin. The bell above the door rang and the room was empty again. Luca sighed. She tilted her head and pictured him wearing a dress. She'd been so worried about Freddy and Ana having sex under her roof but maybe the whole time they'd been raiding her wardrobe. She swallowed.

'Business has got to pick up soon,' he said. 'All these new coffee shops are killing us.'

'People choose quality in the end,' she said slowly. 'Trends become old news quickly.'

He shrugged and ground the coffee beans. The machine whirred brutally.

'Wolfie and Mona are at the hospital today,' he said over the noise. 'They won't be back before you finish. Wolfie said to tell you there's cash on the sideboard.' He topped up her espresso with hot water.

'How's she been?'

'Good some days, bad others. How's Ana? We didn't see her this weekend.'

'She was studying. Can you believe it? I don't even have to nag.'

She took a sip of her coffee. It was strong and sweet but she couldn't linger here now that she'd invaded Freddy's world as well.

'Ana's a good girl,' Luca was saying. 'Since he fell out with Patrick, Freddy's always in his room. Not even playing football. I pray he's studying but who knows. He's so uncommunicative.'

She shrugged and shook her head. She wouldn't know where to begin with boys. She took another gulp of coffee and burned the roof of her mouth. Do Wolfie and Mona's house, she told herself, then you can read another page – just one. Then stop. Don't tempt fate. She finished up her coffee, paid the bill, and leaned across the counter to peck Luca on the cheek. He smelled wonderful, like zesty Italian cologne. Elena was a lucky woman.

Outside, the sun was in full force. She took the long way to Wolfie and Mona's and circled the lake. A pair of white swans swam close to the bank, stately and gentle, four cygnets in their wake. The weeping willows were plump with flowers. Young children swung on the low branches of old oaks, their mothers watching and chatting.

Wolfie's house was old, with a stiff lock that groaned as she opened it. Thirty pounds and a note were next to an overflowing fruit bowl.

Dearest Veronica

Sorry to miss you today but we're at a hospital appointment. If you find what Mona has done with the TV remote there's a tub of egg mayo with your name on it.

Wolfie

Stickmen always punctuated Wolfie's notes. This one featured a crudely drawn woman clutching a tiny remote control. Mona moved all kinds of things around the house. Veronica once found the pestle and mortar in the freezer, and a pepper grinder in Wolfie's smoking shed, stinking of salmon. Over the past few months, the Post-it notes had multiplied. Bright squares of pink, green, yellow and orange, all covered with stickmen and sentence-long reminders: *This is where your reading glasses are kept*; *your hairbrush lives here*. Mona's latest thing was picking flowers from the garden and telling Wolfie they were for Henry, her first love. Once, through a crack in the living-room door, Veronica had seen him pluck the petals and throw them on the floor. 'Who am I, darling?' he'd whispered. 'Tell me who I am.' He stopped when Mona started crying. Poor Wolfie. As if those two hadn't already been through enough. She wished he'd get some help if he wasn't going to put her in a care home.

Although she was fond of them both, she was also glad the house was empty today. She usually preferred it that way, when no one's eyes bounced off her, either embarrassed or unseeing, or glancing at her sideways like a dieter looks at a fridge. She could be alone with her thoughts while she cleaned, powering through rooms full of furniture, vases, paintings, inventing a history behind each object, what they might mean to their owners. She felt the full size of a house without people in it. Especially bedrooms with great big beds no one slept in. She imagined her family's things in there – a room each for the girls, en suite bathrooms too. No screaming when the hot water ran cold. No damp. To be home and not know if someone else was there. If she could give the kids just one thing it would be space.

Work took longer with a heavy heart. She made her way round the house, desperate to get reading again. She had to know more. The bathroom was last but still there was no sign of the remote control. She checked the medicine cabinet above the basin. Rows of supplements seemed to multiply by the week. Olive-leaf extract, zinc, magnesium, B6, B12, folate, omega 3, vitamin D. The remote was there, stuffed behind a packet of adult nappies – that was new. She whispered a quick prayer for

Mona, and then poured a stream of bleach into the toilet, scrubbing around the porcelain until the water foamed. She pulled down the lid, took off her Marigolds and the diary from her bag. She found her place then ran her fingers along the page, scanning the words for *Mama*.

Feb. 12

Freddy's being funny about Valentine's. He thinks we shouldn't support a capitalist opportunity but I said the most anarchist thing would be to actually celebrate when everyone else turns their noses up at it. Plus I—

The front door slammed.

'Veronica?' Wolfie called. 'You still here?'

She snapped the diary shut, flushed the toilet, and grabbed the remote control. Downstairs, Wolfie was putting the kettle on and Mona sat slouched at the kitchen table. She looked crumpled and defeated. Her hair wasn't sitting quite right so Wolfie must have tried to do the curlers that morning. Veronica knew better than to kiss her cheeks hello when she was like that so she presented Wolfie with the remote.

'My angel. *Bake Off* night is saved. Cup of camomile?'

'Already late, Wolfie love, but thank you. Are you OK?'

He nodded his slow nod. 'Did you see the cash by the door?'

'This lady,' Mona said. 'I know her.'

'It's Veronica, our friend who comes to clean the house. She comes every Monday morning.'

'She has a nice voice. I like her voice.' Mona stood. 'Veronica,' she said, reaching out to touch her hair. 'Lovely.'

Wolfie smiled sadly. 'How about we make strudel?'

'I won't eat a thing. Nothing. Nothing, nothing, nothing.'

By the time Veronica packed up her things and stuck her head in the kitchen to say goodbye, Mona's hair was swept back with a red Alice band and she was flour-dusted and kneading away.

'Here,' Wolfie said, handing her a huge Tupperware container of egg mayonnaise. 'For the girls.'

She kissed his cheeks and put the box in her bag. It fitted neatly on top of the diary.

The park pulsed under the heavy afternoon heat. Any attempts at exercise had been abandoned, and the paths were clear. Young couples kissed and kissed on the benches. Groups picnicked in the shade of the trees, blankets spread out, food arranged in piles.

Monty's old house was at the end of the street. Its new owner, Caroline, worked from home. Those clients were always the most difficult, with their fancy trainers, video conferences and nursery schedules. They pretended to be working furiously on laptops but were usually compiling Ocado orders. Or else they wandered listlessly through their home, like they were looking for a lost button. Most of them cleaned everything before she arrived. Caroline couldn't bear to be thought of as unkempt, but she'd also been renovating since she bought the house and there was endless dust, woodchips stuck between floorboards. If Veronica were feeling mean, she'd poke her Marigolds into the dirty corners. She liked to watch Caroline's Botoxed brows try to furrow at the sight of her spoiled rubber gloves.

She pressed the doorbell and listened to the obnoxious chimes, followed by the heavy tread of block heels on a wooden floor. The door swung open and cracked against the wall. 'Shit,' Caroline said, staring at the new brown mark on the paint. A green smoothie was in one hand, the baby balanced on her hip. She looked sallow. 'Veronica,' she breathed. 'Thank goodness you're here. I've got to run some errands and the house is a tip. I'm sure you'll be all right without me for a bit?'

Caroline didn't sound sure. She performed an elaborate neck swivel, gesturing at the house, doing what looked to be a mental scan of every last valuable. Veronica caught a whiff of musky perfume and liquid detergent. Caroline lingered in the doorway. Veronica grasped the baby's pudgy open fist and blew a raspberry on her palm. She gurgled, all blue eyes. So easy to please when they're babies but then they become teenagers. She had to hand it to Caroline, raising a kid alone. The father was a bad man, she'd once said. But money had stuck to her – that must help.

'I'll be fine,' Veronica said, relieved. 'Go. I'll see you when you're back.'

Caroline smiled, grabbed her keys and a nappy bag, laid the baby in the buggy, scanned the hallway again, and then left.

Veronica was usually afraid to dirty the unvarnished wood of Caroline's Danish kitchen table, but today she sat down and took out the diary. She stared at it for a moment, hesitant, and then flicked back through the pages.

Feb. 12

Freddy's being funny about Valentine's. He thinks we shouldn't support a capitalist opportunity but I said the most anarchist thing would be to actually celebrate when everyone else turns their noses up at it. Plus Karly lifted some dresses and gave me three, and now I can give one to Freddy for Valentine's. I sorta feel bad about accepting them because Mama would never forgive me if she knew I had clothes that were nicked. But I couldn't resist. I like being able to gift Freddy things that no one else can. He's gonna light up from the inside tomorrow. I can't wait. No one knows him like I do and no one knows me like he does.

Feb. 14

I knew it! Freddy loves to be cool or whatever, but he couldn't resist Valentine's. He got me tickets to see Panic and a necklace with a little silver pendant in the shape of a pill. He must've saved all his wages from the deli. He said the next bit of saving is to take us to New York. NY! I dream about us there, in CBGB's, even though it closed ages ago, watching Duck Sick play like we did the first night we did it, except everything is louder and the crowd are proper cool and we're drinking those blue cans of PBR not Stella. I can see it all so clearly. Freddy in a tight black dress, me with my head shaved so I don't have to style it. Just flying out the door all the time, running late for the next thing.

She closed the diary. The disappointment gripped her. She'd tempted fate and there it was: her daughter had chosen a thief for a best friend, and now she was wearing stolen clothes. Veronica felt squeezed from the inside, a drum-skin tightness messing with her breath. She'd always thought Karly was a sweet girl – but she should have known better when she'd butchered her nose with that ring. They'd raised their children not to take risks, not to fall in with the wrong crowd. They couldn't afford any mistakes. She remembered the early days, when she used to drill Dawid.

What happens if you come home and I've been arrested?

Repeat the number to call again.

Tell me, where do we keep the cash?

It became a mantra, ingrained in their psyche, but they never discussed what life would be like if she were actually deported. Their family was so settled, so established, so solid, it felt difficult to imagine anyone breaking it up.

And then she was overwhelmed by the image of Dawid's face. Not as it was now, lined and expressive, sometimes a little soft-fleshed from lack of sleep, but when she first saw him winking at her across a basement bar in Soho, too late in the night to be thinking of anything but mischief. She found his voice rough and awkward, repeating 'Sorry, what was that?' each time she couldn't understand his thick accent. He wasn't a handsome man, not like Luca. Dawid had a bulbous nose and broad brow. Skin grey-tinged from all the years he'd been a Tube driver. It wasn't until the night he got drunk and cried a little as he talked about his mother and sister that she knew she loved him. It was two or three months after they met, six months since she'd stayed past her visa. They couldn't afford a proper immigration lawyer. The one officiator they saw was po-faced and heartless and, after that, they got scared and didn't try again. The years went by.

She looked up and took in Caroline's house, remembering when it was Monty's. From the moment she'd entered his place she'd known he was a man who'd never married. Someone who liked attention but not affection. There were rows and rows of suits in the wardrobes. She was as careful with them as she'd be with artwork. You could see the hours of labour and love in each stitch. But there was nothing personal lying around for someone to discover. No apologetic notes to a loved one, or messages about picking up eggs. No baggies of cocaine, or a drawer of dildos. Just one photograph of a young man that may or may not have been him. When he died, he'd left instructions to divide everything he owned between Wolfie and Mona, and Oxfam, and to give his tailoring kit to the boy who delivered his takeout each evening. Had Monty taken any risks in his life, or had he always held back?

Ana was reckless and selfish. But then she thought – my daughter's in love. In *love*. And, despite herself, she smiled.

She caught the 388 bus to Liverpool Street station and met Valentina and Sofia to help on a student house deep-clean. After the hazy calm of the park, she was dazzled as the three of them joined the stream of bodies in their bid to push through the hot crush to the Circle line. She blinked in the synthetic light. The train pulled in, the breeze cool on her sweaty neck.

Someone had left a newspaper on the seat and she turned to the property pages. Although it was full of wild lifestyle photographs – thin blonde women caressing fridges, shirtless men in home gyms, girls with lipstick mouths wrapped around burgers – the houses were incredible. Three storeys, high ceilings, original fireplaces, all the latest in-home technology, and on quiet, leafy streets near good schools. Valentina and Sofia tried to snap the pages shut. 'Boring, cariño!' they said. Maybe it was too much for them to have that kind of luxury thrust in their faces. They pulled out the pages of celebrity gossip, dropped their heads to pore over who'd had a meltdown and where, the latest nipple flash. 'Vee, Vee, look at this one,' Sofia said. 'See where the surgery crashed her face.'

Veronica kept reading the supplement and imagined her family's smiling faces sitting around those huge kitchen tables. One day they'd have that kind of life. She put the paper down and looked at Valentina – twenty years old and studying the celebrity pages for clues to how her life would look when it really started. Did everyone think that way? Was even Rose waiting for another chapter to unfold?

'Why so quiet?' Valentina asked.

Veronica pulled out the diary, turning it in her hands. How many more secrets behind that lurid green cover?

She didn't need to know. The diary would slot neatly back into place behind the radiator. It was a good hiding place. She'd go to Ana's bedroom, fling open the wardrobe, search past the heap of shoes, the jumble of sweaters and jeans. And then there they would be: at the end of one rail, all pushed together, a stack of dresses she wouldn't recognize. She'd gather them up, space out the hangers, and then walk the dresses down to the charity shop. There would be a girl out there, maybe a couple of years older than Ana, who'd have spent her whole day looking for the perfect dress for her date. Or maybe she had plans to travel somewhere hot that summer and wanted to impress on the dance floor of a European disco, hoping to catch the eye of someone with a lovely face, someone who winked at her too late in the night to be thinking of anything but mischief. Smiling, Veronica would hand the dresses to the girl behind the counter so their rightful wearer could claim them, so the new owner could go back to the life they should have been living. Ana would have to wait a little longer for her next chapter.

'Girls, I'm sorry. I need to go. It's Ana. Will you be OK without me?'

They nodded solemnly, kissed her hot cheeks, and she dashed out at the next station. She looked around for the right platform to get her home, studying the loop of the Circle line. She wasn't sure if she was going to or from something.

July

Windows

After the second stroke, what bothered Rose most was losing her way with speech. She used to perform acrobatics with verbs, weave adjectives into exquisite phrases. But now the best words were lodged in her throat and needed levering out. Without the sentences they were redundant. Flat. It was far worse than the numbness in her left arm, or even the shameful thickening of her ballet-dancer frame, something she thought would never happen. So she'd made it to eighty-six. What for? Soon Lottie would arrive with the moving men. And that was that.

The morning had been stifling hot, and she had let it dwindle by watching the boy in the opposite house through her window. Freddy, that was his name. She'd heard his mum yelling for him to come down from the roof enough times. He'd spent the last couple of hours slumped on the edge of his bed, phone in hand. He stared at it with fixed, adoring intensity. She couldn't figure out what held his attention. He looked like the handsome man in that Athena poster, cradling his phone as if it were a baby. Though he must be far too young to remember that ad campaign. Her youngest daughter had the poster tacked to her bedroom wall all through her thorny puberty. Lottie, the mistake she had made at forty. How young forty seemed now, when there were always bruises on her hands, arms, calves, hips. Pale purple. They never made it to the yellow-green stage because they didn't heal. Her skin had become like paper – no, papyrus. Ancient.

The boy was on his feet now, still transfixed by the phone as he uncoiled his body. She could almost hear the pop-pop of his back muscles adjusting. He was tall for a young lad. Lithe yet composed, as if he were about to break into dance. There was potential there; she still had the eye for it. He put the phone on his bed and peeled off a navy T-shirt, revealing tanned olive skin and jutting shoulders. The outline of arm muscles visible, though he held his hands all wrong. Awkward, like many boys his age.

If she'd had sons it would have been easier. They say men marry and leave their mothers, while girls – girls you have forever. But she'd never met more self-interested people than her daughters. You couldn't pay her to spend forever with them. If it hadn't been for her pregnancies, those first two, only ten months apart, she would have become a prima ballerina – not a teacher. As it was, the certificates and trophies on her bookcase trailed off after '62. The books were going to take an age to pack. It was a hefty collection. Marion, the middle one, loved reading when she was little. It delighted Rose and horrified Vince. But the child grew up to be clumsy. That was a real failure. How she'd raised an ungainly daughter, she'd never know. She herself had hopped and spun through life. *Pas de chat. Jeté, jeté.* All elegance. Equanimity. Born pirouetting, folks on their street would tell her. Not even the crack of her father's belt threatened her poise. And when she was discovered at the church ballet recital, well, then he had nothing on her. She made her own way with scholarships and sweat. Oh yes, she was slim and alive as a child, not like Marion, hunched over a crime novel – you couldn't even find the best words in those. As for her eldest, sleeping with her own sex: she was no longer family.

Then, nearly twenty years later, Lottie. Chomping down on her irritated, sore breasts with early-formed teeth. Cracked skin and threads of blood. Those years – nothing but a blur of fatigue. Marion and Agnes all grown up but still clamouring for attention, unable to see beyond themselves. All me me me.

Children complicated things. Somehow slowed time but made you hurry through it too. Years of merciless pacing with the pram. All doctors' offices looked the same. Sniffles, rashes, fevers. The monotony and the vomit. Life grey-washed. Neutralized. Then the teenage drama. People coming in and out – nothing but shadows. Dim images. Vince's laugh somewhere in the background late at night when he got in, a little drunk, or just bone-tired. She was always trying to figure out how to halt the movement of her body through time as, minute by minute, her real life was ticking by somewhere, not waiting for her to reclaim it.

When the fog finally cleared, she was fifty-six and Vince was gone, taking one of her ballet students with him. Predictable, his weakness for youth.

Now Marion lived in some godforsaken country, and she was stuck with Lottie fussing round her. The girl made terrible decisions. Working in a florist, for heaven's sake. What was the point of her education if she was going to end up in a shop? She wasn't even interested in the reasons her customers were buying the flowers in the first place and that was the best bit. Not a hint of curiosity about her. And she'd married an *Arab*. How long left before Lottie turned up? Time was harder and harder to quantify.

She turned her attention back to the scene from her window. The boy was still stretching in his bedroom. He was framed by the trees outside, the edges of their leaves beginning to brown in the heat. Touching his toes.

Extending his arms. He really knew how to hold himself. She might even miss the boy when she left. The strange way about him. His earnest face as he waited to make his way through the world – even if it was a feminine way. Her phone was ringing but whoever it was ought to have known better. She should have unplugged it weeks ago. It was useless to her now.

Until recently, every evening she'd done her hair in curlers, put on talc after she bathed, and ironed her nightdress in case that night was the night. How horrid to be discovered in disarray. She hoped they'd be quick about it too – nothing worse than a bad smell to accompany your passing. Though she supposed now it would be Lottie who found her. Marion sent postcards, of course: *All well here, sun shining, promotion at work, kids walking now.* She kept them in an old box at the bottom of her wardrobe. She used to imagine them sorting it all out after she'd gone, how long it would take. Lottie was going to get a shock when she arrived today. Not even the damned cleaner knew how much she'd hidden away over the years: she kept the wardrobes and cupboards locked, not only to deter roaming hands, but to keep their contents from bulging, spilling out into the room.

Before the first stroke she took the bus to Stratford every Friday, a modest bundle of crisp notes in her cracked leather wallet. Thirty-five long minutes. Babies crying, too-loud conversations, the smell of fried chicken from greasy boxes and the sucking sound of bones being pulled clean. But when the bus arrived at the entrance of the sprawling shopping centre, her heartbeat would quicken. Three storeys, an all-glass masterpiece – something the modern world had got right.

Marks and Spencer, her Achilles heel. Even the sight of a stranger carrying that green and gold plastic bag sent a thrill through her. The shop was spread across two levels. Food hall on the ground, beauty and clothing on the first. She'd start at the top and work her way down. Scooping out the tester pots of rich creams and foaming lotions, smearing it across her skin. Feeling it sink in. Sniff sniff. Roses, violets, or something fruity like pineapples.

And it was as if the clothes were expecting her, so perfectly did they hang on the rails, evenly spaced, all in a row – the way her students had lined up at the barre, poised and awaiting instruction. She'd run her fingertips over the fabric. Dresses, trousers, skirts, swaying beneath her touch. She waved away anyone who offered her help with sizes. No need to try anything on. It was not the wearing of the thing: it was looking at something, then possessing it. All those flesh-coloured stockings never worn. Packs and packs of lace panties of no use. Often she'd forget what she bought and then, at home, there'd be two or three of the same jumpers neatly folded on the shelf, mocking her memory. At least she had an established style. Red was her colour. Pillar-box, crimson, burgundy. It played to her pale skin, popped the green of her eyes. Round neck. Sometimes a smart cable-knit running from shoulder to waist – she liked the ordered intricacy of it. Never a fussy print. She scoffed. at florals – pastels too, for that matter. Bold colour and a simple cut – all a woman needed.

Then a hand on the escalator rail; a moment to attune to its gentle judder. Fresh produce picked for its colour. She liked to open the fridge to a nice display. Though she cared little for the taste of things. A lot of it ended up in the bin. A throwback to the dancing days, she supposed, when everything she ate in one day could fit on a single plate. All those nights when she'd lain in bed, palming her concave belly, stroking the line of each rib, pushing into the dip of her waist, looking forward to morning when she could eat a hard-boiled egg – the whole day ahead of her to burn its ninety calories. Now her freezer chest was full of old meat, bags of pureed spinach, loaves of bread – some, decades old. In the cupboards – labels peeling, tins rusting. For the years her old friend Audrey was sick, she had picked up her food too. Yogurts, porridge oats, soup, fruit compote. Everything soft, easy to spoon, easy to swallow. Her friend's eyes rolling to the back of her head with the pleasure of something sugary. The colour of her skin like old ivory, yellowing and past its glory. They'd played cards for hours. She'd bought dozens and dozens of decks – Aspinal, Christian Lacroix – though they'd only ever used the same one. She never let Audrey win.

Yes, she had seen death in all its forms. Peaceful and relieved. Brutal and struggling. The passing of parents, aunts, uncles and friends had afforded her an opportunity to apply what she'd learned to her own ending. She vowed to be graceful like her mother, who lay down with her cancer and let it wash over her until it washed her away. Certainly she would not be bitter and resentful like Audrey, all wild-eyed and resisting, refusing reality right until the last breath. No no, it really wouldn't do to go out kicking and screaming like a newborn.

She read the obituaries religiously, triumphant at having evaded them for so long. Funerals were a lesson in magnanimity and style. She jotted down ideas in a little notebook, affectionately christened *The Death Diary*, as if planning a party, or organizing the week's shopping list. She'd wanted to play 'Raglan Road' during the ceremony but too many people had the same idea. It was taking time to find a new song. Lilies were clichéd so the church should be filled with white roses. The trend for not wearing black was disrespectful – her mourners should dress appropriately for the occasion. This way, not even her daughters could mess things up. It was a shame she wouldn't be able to see the finished effect.

The problem: she was running out of people to invite.

She supposed some might call her pragmatic. But, truth be told, the older she got, the less she accepted the inevitability of her own death. Recently, she had begun to imagine that if she gathered enough knowledge about life, it might allow her to keep living – like earning points on a game show to qualify for the next round.

Her thighs were sticky with sweat, and she peeled her cotton skirt from the leather of Vince's armchair, the one he never came back to pick up. Would the moving men be rough with it? Drop it down the stairs? Maybe that'd be a blessing. She shifted her weight again. Some days, she swore she could still see the imprint of his heavy backside on the worn brown leather. When they met, he said he was an entrepreneur but by the time she discovered he was really just a wheeler-dealer they were married. There was no faffing about in those days with long engagements. You met someone local who'd *do* and you settled down. The whole of east London smelled like tanning leather then and the vinegar the Jews used when they cooked. She thought they were bad enough, but now the street corners echoed with Muslims. Their cloaked silhouettes gave her the shivers.

She first saw Vince at the deli, the Jewish one she never usually went to, but Ralph's place had closed early that day and she needed coffee. He was sitting at the counter, chestnut hair slicked back with pomade, a long laugh – one, two, three Mississippi's worth – enough time for her to notice his broad shoulders. She liked his impish smile, the way the hairs on the crown of his head stuck up even though he'd clearly gone to lengths to stop them. He knew that once you made a girl laugh, really belly-laugh, then she'd be yours forever. His eyes were so pale, like the plug had been pulled on the colour, and if they were the windows to the soul like everybody said, why – she should have known sooner.

But sex thoughts drifted over her, even now. At least there was one thing he was good at. The way they said sorry with their bodies after the fights. Undoing spiteful words with each piece of clothing removed. For a long time they muddled through this way, working and squabbling, making ends meet. Once a month he'd take her down to the Hackney Empire for a variety show, the double seats at the back so she could get into the crook of his arm and forget she had children for a few hours. He sat with his legs sprawled. Wherever he went, he always appeared to be comfortable. There was something smug about it.

It wasn't becoming for a woman to lose her temper. She knew that. The anger marred her face, her nostrils flaring so much she could feel the muscles expanding. And spitting a little when she shouted, she knew she did that too. But it was provocation, not her nature. It was what he *did* to her. She couldn't assume responsibility for all of it. He was no delight to live with either.

No conversation. Just a note on the kitchen table. Strange choice for a man who loved to talk the talk. She couldn't even remember ever having seen a pen in his hand. It used to be that divorce was only for rich folk.

The girls still had him in their lives – his new wife too, though she didn't let them breathe either name in her house. She never pandered to her daughters. Spoke to them as adults from the day they were born. So after Vince left, she just kept going. No change in routine. No drama. No deep-clean. No exorcism. All was the same except for mealtimes. Those were impossible. Cooking had never been anything but a chore, and without a cross-armed man waiting at the table she found she'd no desire to get better. Hot dogs out of the packet and tinned peas for dinner. Newspaper-wrapped fish 'n' chips if she really couldn't be bothered.

She stopped worrying about crossing the road properly – life was chance.

When he left, she'd moved Vince's armchair from its position by the fireplace to the window – her favourite feature of the flat. A beautiful wide bay, third floor, high enough to see the whole street and into her neighbours' bedrooms opposite whenever she swept aside the netting. The widening gaps between the frame and pane whistled with the draught, year-round. There was a blanket on the armchair even now, in the summer. She was always cold.

The fireplace in the corner had clogged up from years of use, specks of soot dropping sometimes on to the tiles, a sour odour coming from somewhere in its depth. Vince never wanted to pay for a chimney sweep and later she found she couldn't form new habits.

The flat was a gift, left to her by a spinster aunt who, like her, left Ireland and came to London in search of – love? Work? Peace? Her aunt had found at least one of those things and bought the flat with her wages as a schoolmistress. It had generous ceilings and three bedrooms, but no one wanted to live round here in those times. Too many Jews. When she moved in, she had nothing but a tea chest, a hurricane lamp and a camp bed. But she'd made it a home, adding pieces of furniture from the second-hand dealer in the arches over the years, before he got too pricey. Lovely porcelain elephants for the bookshelves. Solid-silver candlesticks, heavy square bases with slim stems. Ruffled lampshades in block colours. The flat was always hers. Even when Vince pranced about like a king, handing her his washing, waiting for dinner, spoiling the furniture with cigarette burns. Each corner she carefully dusted. Bleach. Brasso. Citric acid. Why, she'd been scrubbing floors since she was four years old! Having to get help now from that cleaner was an embarrassment. She should've looked after her joints better when she was dancing. Stretched harder. Longer. But she was impatient – always on the go. Rushing out. The next thing!

Back when her left arm was still working, the window was where she came to sew. Skim the paper. She used to excel at the Sunday crossword. All her lovely words. And in her bedroom she had a view of the park. People told her she was lucky – all that nature, they said. So rare in the city. They would name the trees that bordered her vista, or the birds that sang in the mornings. But in all honesty, she cared little for the park. In fact, she rarely even walked through it. Never noticed the changing seasons. Summer or winter sprang up on her like hiding children. Boo! No, it was people-watching that was the best thing.

The hushed hours were her favourite. Dawn mornings, when sleepy bodies pushed themselves to walk faster – get to the car, turn on the engine, seat belt on. Or hurrying for the bus, great clusters of them at the stop. What they were wearing that day changed the way they walked. Brisk in skirt suits. Slouching in jeans. So quiet in their busyness, some still chewing breakfast, buttered toast in hand. Their faces drooping at the jaw, or tense, excited. Staring into their mobile phones, headphones in, absorbed in the private countdown of minutes before work began.

The window was level with a street lamp, an old caged one, though it threw out a horrid orange light these days. Another person might have found it obtrusive, but it was perfect for night-time watching. The whisky-heavy walks of men leaving the pub. Neighbours illuminated as they moved from room to room. The size of their bed and where they positioned it said a lot about a person. Close to the door betrayed a sense of panic. In the centre meant they did it a lot. The number of decorative cushions was also revealing. The new mother across the street removed nine cushions from her bed each night, retiring them to a huge wooden chest until morning. Nine! What vanity.

At midnight, after the last bus of the day left with the nightcap drinkers, a homeless couple slept on the bus-stop bench. No doubt they'd been kicked out of the park when the gates were locked. An unpleasant fate for sure, but things like that really brought down house prices.

And then the arguments. She had a sweet spot for those. Others' open windows were a delight. Her neighbours didn't seem to realize how well the sound travelled across the street. The power of a person's pause – where they chose to stop and think and reword something, to be more cruel, or kinder, depending. The frequency of wails – one pitch for despair, another for pain. She knew more than anyone about this neighbourhood.

Did anyone ever look back at her? She never lost the desire to be watched all the time, could not forget the pleasure of being appraised and applauded. She'd learned early on it was the little details that mattered. The fan of her fingers in arabesque, nail ridges buffed smooth, cuticles trimmed and oiled. Neck arched. She could be fish. Water. Spirit. The physical sacrifices a dancer endured to transform into weightlessness. Her poor, poor feet, toes bent and curled from point work. When Vince really wanted to annoy her, he'd grab a foot and ram her crabbed toes in his mouth. But she knew how to take care of the rest of her body. At night, she smoothed her hair away from her eyes, coyly tucking it behind her ear. She could make satin ripple. She had turned heads. And sometimes people said she was closed, not tremendously giving, and yes, that was true. She preferred being on the receiving end. Her face stayed beautiful for a long time, even though she'd worked outside on the farm for too many hours as a child and wrinkled sooner than most. She was never haggard, though. Not crumpled like some of her friends whose features had morphed into the shape of wet laundry. Her lines were like etchings – intricate and delicate. In the park café, there was a young artist who liked to draw her face. She'd sat for hours, content to be under the woman's gaze. She felt herself radiating. *You look like Margot Fonteyn*, the artist said. No, no, she replied, more like Galina Ulanova with her lovely small nose. It was a shame she was too petite to ever try and make it as a model.

But now she was fascinated by what people did when they thought no one was looking. How they gritted their teeth and bit their lips. How their faces drooped with sadness when they switched off smiles. No one ever thought you were watching, or judging.

Over the years, the streets around the park filled up with the well-to-dos. Architects, advertising people, lawyers. A couple of actors who'd been on the West End stage. They were people with suits and dresses that fitted like a second skin. No wrinkles or pulling. It felt good to live alongside the successful, drink cappuccino next to their urgent conversations in the café. Such shrill, energetic ways of talking. Simple things in the village became more elegant. Italian meats curing in the window of the Jewish deli, shelves of biscotti, dried pasta. Even the chippie got a makeover – shiny black tiles and dim lighting and young, good-looking couples at tables, gold glinting in their ears and on their wrists. An organic wine shop! But she couldn't afford the fishmonger or the butcher's any more. Fourteen pounds for a bit of smoked gammon? Or the florist where Lottie worked, come to think of it. She used to go to Columbia Road on a Sunday, buy a posy of whatever was in season for a couple of pounds. But it was too far to walk now, and packed with foreigners taking pictures. Huge crowds of them never buying a thing. Snap-snapping with their oversized cameras. It was a new world.

She used to hear all the gossip at the shops. Who'd been in hospital and who'd run off with a new fancy man. Especially the grocer's, while you waited for butter to be chopped from the block, or cheese cut with wire from the wheel. These days, Lottie ordered food for her on a computer and the groceries appeared at her door-step. The accents of the delivery boys were unintelligible. No one cared to sniff the top of melons for ripeness, or check tins for dents. She had little appetite anyway. Boiled eggs did her fine. These days she allowed herself to have two.

But she didn't resent the new kind of folk who moved into the park. She admired how they'd thrown away their parents' world. Her childhood was no picnic. Chores from five in the morning, a full day at school. Being told she was lucky to have an education. Bedbug-scratching meant she couldn't concentrate on a thing the teacher said. Hours of ballet lessons at church. So, good for them, those well-to-dos, having all that space to call their own.

It hadn't escaped her attention, however, that accom-panying the manicured front lawns and glossy paint jobs were as many snarls and snaps in the street as before. Drunken fights outside the pub. Sometimes the sound of a body slamming against a wall. It didn't seem to matter how wealthy the neighbourhood became. People didn't change.

And sometime before Christmas there was that bald man on a scooter – it was his shining head beneath the moon that first caught her eye. It made his skin an unnatural, foaming white, the way Cif goes when it's brushed with a Brillo pad. He looked big, bulky and tall, even though he was sitting down. Only wearing a grey jumper, blue jeans. He must have been freezing. It was a while before she realized he was following a younger man down the street, and then on foot through the gate into the park. She couldn't see what he was carrying, but she did notice that he kept a tight fist. It was a rare occasion when weather stuck in her mind, but she remembered the way their breath transformed into frosty plumes in front of them. The youth's fast and small. The older man's large and slower, like a puffing dragon.

When she heard about it on the radio, she wasn't sure why she kept quiet. And later, when Lottie brought it up, she shrugged. She didn't want to look at the photograph of the boy's torso and legs. That expressionless coma face. She didn't understand why they had to show it on television.

'Mum?'

Rose turned away from the window. Lottie's fingers curved around the doorframe before the rest of her appeared. She had the same bony fingers, as if designed to jab someone in the chest to emphasize a point. You – jab – must – listen – jab – to – me. Her mild blue eyes often distorted with fury, lending them an intensity she didn't really deserve. She had a sensuous, generous mouth, though, she'd give her that.

'Mum! There you are. Did you not hear me come in? The moving guys are on their way. I know you're angry. But we talked about this – sorry, we wrote all of this down and—'

Rose turned her back and faced the window again. Lottie never made eye contact when she spoke to her. It was infuriating. The boy was still in his bedroom, stripped down to his shorts now. He placed one foot forward, hips swaying. Lips pouting. Deadpan expression. One step, two step, three step. A catwalk-style walk. Up and down he went, then stopped to study the phone again. And then she realized: he was trying to walk like a woman. Her dry lips parted to laugh but all that came out was an ugly rasp. She wanted to rush across the road and correct his posture. He was doing it all wrong. The hips needed to sashay more. *Make your back straight as a rod*, she'd tell him. *Keep your eyes forwards. Focus!*

'Mum, where's your notebook? Write it down. Tell me how you're feeling.'

Lottie set the post down beside her. A pile of bills and circulars, maybe a delayed postcard from Marion. How she hated that damn notebook! She turned and gestured that it was on the arm of the couch. She took the pad and with a black Sharpie wrote, *I'm not moving in with that Arab*. She pushed the page back towards her daughter.

'Christ, Mum, we've been married for years. When are you going to accept that? We've made your room look lovely. All your books, the tartan blanket, pictures of Grandad and Grandma. There's a kettle in there to make a brew. The girls went out this morning and picked you flowers. It's going to be good, Mum. We're going to make this work. All of us. A proper family.'

Rose turned her back on her daughter. The street was filling with people. It must have been lunchtime. The lesbian from the cul-de-sac flats always went to the Jewish deli and walked to the park with what looked like a salt-beef bagel. The strange but beautiful hippie ate at the vegetarian café if she wasn't working. No habits went unnoticed. She knew who was kind, or stroppy, or ungrateful. Which marriages had made the grade and which had crumbled. This was *her* street. How could she bear knowing strangers were going to be renting her home? Walking through her bedroom. Changing the layout. Their dirty fingers smudging the windows. Hairs clogging the drain in the bathtub. Children picking their noses, smearing snot under the kitchen table. It was true her body had given up. It was to be expected. But this place was solid. Had endured a hundred years more than her.

'It isn't safe for you to be alone here,' Lottie continued. 'Not after the last stroke. This is the best way. The kids are so excited to have you around. Won't that be nice?'

Lottie disappeared into the bathroom. From the clattering, Rose supposed she was beginning to pack in there.

Towels. Talcum powder. The boxes of old ballet slip-
pers which had ended up in the boiler cabinet. Roughly
shoving them into a bag, no doubt. Lottie didn't have a
delicate touch. How little her daughter knew her if she
thought the grandchildren would be an incentive to leave
her home. She belonged here, where it was appropriate to
be silent. Where life went on.

'Christ, it's so stuffy in here,' Lottie said, striding back
into the room. She opened the window.

August

After You

When the last person left the basement shrine, Alice blew across the row of tea lights burning beneath the bronze Buddha statue. The flames shuddered then hissed. They seemed to go out one by one, neatly, like synchronized divers, but that couldn't have been true. She allowed the incense to keep burning in the sand-filled cup, nyam chang smoke spiralling around her as she restacked the cushions and adjusted the pile of mats. The room was painted dark green and when the incense was lit she thought of a forest burning, flames licking leaves. She breathed in, breathed out. Stretched, bending first backwards then forwards like an accordion. That was nice. The flowers would keep for another day or two. She bowed and pressed her hands together so they were pointing towards the Buddha then straightened, tucking her cream silk camisole back into the waistband of her faded Levi's. She could not remember what prompted her to buy the thing and now it didn't even fit; all her clothes had become looser recently, as if conspiring to run away from her body.

At the beginning of the year, the chairman had launched a successful PR campaign directed at the under thirties. The building had swollen with faces framed by oversized glasses and layered black cashmere. They'd opened up the basement to accommodate more meditation classes and, just when Alice was about to resign, the chairman suggested extra teaching would be a good way for her to begin healing. In the meeting, she'd found herself suddenly voiceless, acquiescing with a submissive nod. She'd been lumbered with the Saturday-morning sessions. The incense never quite disguised the damp. She could feel her lungs eroding. Let them rot.

An eight o'clock start drew the restless. Those thankful to rise early and end a night of tossing and turning. The overambitious who fitted in an hour's run before class. Now that it was summer, the windowless space took on a swampy feel, the air humid and still, layers of natural deodorant dissolving into a sharp tang. Sweat tickled the back of her neck, slicking her hair to her body. Most of her class fell asleep within the first ten minutes, faces gentle and settled, expressing half-dreams until snores punctuated the silence. She had a soft spot for the sleepers. She liked how the feeling of the room developed over the hour. Observing rows of students kneeling or cross-legged before her, how their bodies changed from bolt upright, seemingly self-possessed, to swaying, or leaning forward into whatever thoughts were arising. A sneeze, a cough, a scratch, a bubbly fart. She should keep her eyes closed but it was too tempting.

Occasionally, she tried to meditate along with them, but the responsibility of ringing the bells for each stage of the process required her to stay alert. She marked every fifteen minutes. Sometimes this was soothing so she counted the seconds too. She liked to linger on every tenth number, drawing out the *ty* sound in her head. Twen-*ty*, thir-*ty*, for-*ty*. Mostly it was a challenge to keep track. Since she had left Malik, time seemed to move at a different pace, like someone had loosened a cog in the back of a clock. There were longer gaps now between ticks and tocks. She walked slower. Ate languorously. Nothing to rush for, everything to savour.

She took another look at the Buddha, this time face on. His pronounced angel's touch, that deep channel chiselled between a straight nose and full mouth, was mesmerizing. The statue was new, larger than the others in the building but holding the same sanguine lotus pose. His expression was watchful, without menace. It ignited something confrontational in her and she tried to outstare him, or stare him down. Eyeballing the Buddha was a bad habit which had become worse in recent months. She wanted him to acknowledge her devotion, her deference.

She wasn't asking for much – the lifting of her mood, or some other sign that her efforts were paying off. But she was still waiting. The bastard. Hadn't she done enough of that with Malik's cirrhosis? The yellowish skin on his face loose over sharp bones, the alopecia making a glowing dome of his head. She so visibly younger than him, even when two white streaks appeared in her hair, framing her face like a slipped halo sliced in half.

She flicked off the lights, shut the shrine-room door, and climbed the stairs barefoot, sandals and bag dangling from her hand. There had been a light rain last night, and the small courtyard at the front of the centre looked scrubbed and gleaming. White hollyhocks and searing blue spires of delphiniums shot up from terracotta pots. A few bowles mauve were nosing their way out of the earth, and a second flush of purple downy clematis scrambled across the red brick. Nature was so alive. It exhausted her.

Students from her class were chatting over cups of lemon barley water. A few thanked her and she smiled. She noticed Bettie doing up her shoes on the bench's edge. A squirrel was balanced on a branch above her head, clutching a knot of croissant. It looked at her then scuttled up the tree.

Alice took a seat beside Bettie. She was one of her favourites, a sporadic student, but her questions about patience and boredom in meditation were pertinent and interesting – the same questions she herself used to ponder. Bettie never fell asleep in her classes. In fact, she didn't think Bettie switched off at all. She was always frowning.

'I was hoping to catch you,' Bettie said. She wound a black hair around her finger. 'Mia's pregnant. Four months now. We're moving to Surrey, to be near her parents.'

Alice smiled and congratulated her.

'We're having a girl, thank God. I got a job in the local comprehensive. I did a trial lesson, and kids there seem to not mind learning – it was unnerving.' She laughed.

Alice had heard a lot about Bettie's work, the violent outbreaks, endless administration, lack of funding. Kids who wouldn't respond to anything – kindness, humour, threat. She wondered if her own patience would have extended to raising teenagers. She hugged Bettie and hoped she'd keep meditating. More and more of her older students were leaving the city, tired of rising house prices. She'd been lucky; Malik had bought their house outright after selling his art gallery in the nineties.

Opening the gate, she headed towards home. People on the streets walked with lowered heads, following a map on their phone or typing with one thumb. She envied their simple absorption. She took some sunscreen from her bag, rubbed lotion on to her shoulders. She went the long way round, passing the Italian café where she bought biscotti, the yoga studio, until she reached

Bethnal Green Gardens and stopped by the memorial for the Tube disaster. The concrete statue had stood unfinished for decades but had recently been completed. She touched the steel plaque on the angular plinth, feeling the etched names of those who'd died. Edna, Alfred, Elsie. As old as sixty-nine, as young as fourteen months. William, Clara, Mary. It had been a terrible mistake. The air-raid siren sounding, not from bombs, as people thought, but from the discharge of anti-aircraft rockets fired from Victoria Park. Hundreds piled into the tube station to take shelter until a woman tripped and others fell around her. Panic caused a stampede – three hundred crushed. But the tragedy was kept quiet during the war years. For morale, they said. The memorial was named *Stairway to Heaven* but had always been missing the stairway. It rose now, finely carved wooden steps that led nowhere.

Not being able to get away was the worst thing. Malik had sensed her increased distance from him and became petty when he could no longer raise his fists. He snooped through her bureau and stole her favourite socks. He'd offer to make toast for them and then burn hers. Once he drew a lipstick penis on her face while she slept. She retaliated by becoming more and more engrossed in her own body. She doubled the hours spent at yoga, purchased expensive exfoliating scrubs, sloughing away dead skin cells, watching the grey mush clog up the drain. She took long baths, cloudy with Epsom salts. Lavished her skin with oils – rosehip, marula, squalane – and ran the excess along the ends of her hair. She'd never looked better. She would hold him, feeling grateful they'd never had a child, and stroke his smooth head until he leaned into the crook of her neck and his breath trembled across her skin. It was the sounds – the sounds she hated the most. The mucus and the wheezing and the rattling. She kept busy with the housekeeping, with cooking soup. Staring into pots of boiled vegetables, the hand blender devastating the soft chunks.

She walked past the park's east gate. It had always been her sanctuary, the reason Malik bought the house in the first place, but after the acid attack last year something ugly had lingered there. It shook her that the attacker still hadn't been caught. The police had recently released another photograph of the victim's face to encourage new information. She'd looked at the image for a long time, his delicate young neck and torso all white blisters, corroded skin. There was a rawness to his expression. Six months in a coma. All that waiting.

But the park was the backbone of her new routine. She'd had to find a way to keep loving her home, to resist feeling like it anchored her to a life that wasn't hers. So, each morning she soaked for twenty minutes in the bath, sipped a decaf coffee, ate a slice of rye toast with two soft-boiled eggs. Then she went to the park and meditated for forty minutes beneath what she considered to be her tree, an ash with sturdy boughs, a great cloud of green leaves, and a gap in the foliage where a branch had fallen.

There was comfort to be found in how well the trees coexisted, in the silent way they communicated with one another, sharing water and nutrients, sending warning signals about droughts and disease. It was a complicated web of kinship, a system without prejudice. The trees were a more reliable community than any she'd participated in herself. So she inserted her body between their strong trunks and beneath the shelter of their canopies: this was how she was putting herself back together.

Inside the house, she dropped her bag on the floor and retrieved her yoga mat from the umbrella bucket in the hallway. The quickest way to get to her tree was through the back garden but this meant walking past Malik's vegetable patch, gardening a hobby he'd taken up when he became too sick to sell art. His green fingers surprised her. She'd come home to crowds of peas, courgettes, potatoes, sometimes even creamy parsnips laid out on their kitchen table like a pirate's haul, waiting for a compliment.

She averted her eyes from the decomposing fruits and vegetables. The smell was earthy, reassuringly rotten. Things pass, go back into the ground, become new again.

The park's wide paths, designed for horse and carriage, were full of speeding bicycles. She passed kissing couples on iron benches, mothers pushing strollers, runners sweating, kids chasing footballs around the grass. Their energy was grotesque. Most of the leaves were still bleached from the summer but a few were darkening, hinting at the auburn to come. The sun blazed. She found a shady spot beneath her ash, unfurled her mat and tucked her legs into a full lotus.

Closing her eyes, she tried to switch off the sound of ringing phones and bicycle bells. She listened to the slight breeze coming over the trees then dropping through the hedges. She willed herself to become interested in her breath, visualizing it first as a silver mist, then as a transparent liquid drawn in through her nostrils and down to her throat, where it rushed into her belly and flowed out again through her nose. In and out. In and out. But then she remembered the absent-minded way Malik used to kiss the outside of her ear. She heard his ragged breath, laboured and wet as if a plastic bag were taped around his head. She felt heavy and hot and tired. She adjusted her posture.

She tried to imagine dropping down into a cool lake, sinking into deep pools of electric calm. But when she reached the bottom Malik was waiting and she was cross. *Please*, she imagined saying to her husband, *you had it coming, all of it.* The image of him smiled back at her. He looked as he did when they first met: so solid, so firm. Stood at his full height he was six foot two. Shoulders broad. So disarming. She could smell his herby green cologne.

Then a blink of a childhood memory. She was paper marbling during an art class at school. A shallow tray filled with water and colourful paints dripped on to its surface. Crisp white paper carefully laid on top, then lifted up, water rolling off until an imprint of the surface was all that was left.

But her mind betrayed her and her focus drifted back to Malik, the memory she tried hardest to avoid and the one which came to her most often. Each time it returned, she saw the whole scene through his eyes, not her own. She'd been wearing her white terrycloth robe that final morning, which she'd later had to bin because of the bloodstains. Her hair halfway from ashy blonde to grey, the robe pulled tightly round her waist, a strip of cotton nightie showing. Bare feet. Her mug had shattered against the bedside table and the milky tea spooled across the surface and seeped into the unmade bed. She bent to fix the sheets – then thought better of it. But she stayed leaning over the mess, not moving for what felt like a very long time. Through Malik's eyes, it was a terrible sight, Alice hunched over like that. The cut-glass ashtray had gashed a hole in the wall and there was a small mound of dust and plasterboard on the polished oak floors.

This time, the last time, hadn't been so bad really, certainly not the worst. But the ferocity with which he threw the ashtray, despite his sickness, had settled it. She couldn't wait till he died. So when she finally stood up straight again she arranged her face to be expressionless, eyes unblinking. No emotion at all. That's when he knew and started bawling. Bawling like a little child. She'd got him out of the house and into a hospice and that was that.

'What're you doing?' a young voice asked.

When Alice opened her eyes, a little girl was crouching inches from her nose. She'd seen the girl in the playground with her mum sometimes, and had admired how they had honey-coloured hair. Up close, Alice reckoned the girl was nine or ten years old, with wide blue eyes, and a cleft chin that gave her a defiant look. Her hair had been twisted into a topknot. The girl tilted her head to the side and repeated the question.

'I was meditating,' Alice said. 'Do you know what that is?'

'Oh.' She swung a pink plastic umbrella. 'You're doing it wrong. Meditating's like this.'

She wriggled free of a panda-shaped backpack which almost eclipsed her and plunged to the ground, folding one skinny leg over the other. She squeezed the pads of her thumb and forefinger together and let out a throaty *om*, frowning in concentration before dropping the sound.

'Wonderful! Where did you learn that?' Alice asked.

'My mum's a nurse. She took me to meditation classes at her hospital.'

'You have a lovely posture. In the meditation I do, we don't say *om* when we're meditating. We try to stay completely silent.'

'That sounds boring.'

'It often is,' Alice laughed.

'Why do it?'

'I suppose it makes me feel calm, like I'm part of nature. And I get to know myself a bit better.'

The girl nodded at her the way adults nod when someone has said something stupid.

'I already know who I am,' she said, and leaned in and fingered the wooden beads snug around Alice's neck. 'They look like pebbles. So pretty.'

'Thank you. You live across the park, don't you? What's your name? I'm Alice.'

'Lydia. Watch me do a handstand.'

She sank her hands in the grass, flipped her body and turned her plimsolls to the sky. Her white vest flapped over her head to reveal a marshmallow belly peeking out from her shorts. Alice resisted tickling her. The rest of her body was all angles and joints. Freckled legs wavered in the air for a moment before she flumped back down on to her feet. Alice thought the girl belonged in wild, bright colours. She would never dress her in white.

'Bravo!' she said, clapping.

Lydia sprang up, stretched and performed a hesitant curtsey. 'Was it good?'

'Perfect. Are your parents nearby?'

She leaned in. 'Can you keep secrets?'

Alice was silent. She was an excellent secret-keeper.

The girl gave her a serious look and then seemed to decide she could be trusted. 'I'm running away from home.'

'Oh no. Why's that?'

'Rupert's dead and it's my dad's fault!'

'Goodness. Who is Rupert?'

'My dog. Yesterday he was sick on the floor but Dad made me go to art club anyway, and when I came home Rupert was gone.'

'That's terrible. I bet your dad is really sad too.'

'Dad's been sad for ages. My brother thinks the dog was his but really he was mine. I walked him. I fed him. Dad told me that Rupert just woke up dead. I hate him. I hate him!' She broke into tears and clutched Alice's knee.

She put her arm around Lydia. The girl felt warm and familiar. Alice smoothed away the sticky stray hairs from her forehead and slipped them back into her bun. It occurred to her that this might not be appropriate. She ignored the desire to pull her on to her lap. She made little shushing sounds.

'I don't normally cry,' Lydia said. 'I normally hold all the water in my eyes, and even when I'm really, really sad I don't let it drop out.'

'Oh, let it drop. A good cry always makes me feel better.'

She didn't cry when Malik actually died, though she'd thought she would. Instead, she was flooded with relief. She felt hopelessly unsentimental. Vibrant and undeniably alive. It was mortifying to realize that she'd had this stone heart inside her the whole time.

Lydia wiped her nose on her arm. 'I'm scared I'm going to forget Rupert,' she said.

Alice looked at the smear of snot on the girl's skin. 'I don't think we forget about the things we love.'

'But what if I do?' Lydia said, scrambling out of Alice's grasp. 'What if everything turns into a big smoosh in my head and then I forget all about him?'

She wrapped her arms around her knees and Alice noticed that they were pink, toasted from the sun.

'Well we do forget a lot of things, but I think it's OK to do that.' Alice played with the small hole at the edge of her yoga mat. 'It can be very peaceful to forget.' She tapped the side of her head. 'The big stuff stays in there.'

It was true – Alice had memories that were stuck inside her like a barbed fish.

'You know what I love most about Rupert? His paws. Not the furry bit, the pink bit. It looks like something that should be on the inside of your body but it's on the outside. Did you have a dog when you were little?'

'No, my dad didn't like dogs.'

'You have to be really weird to not like dogs. Did you have any other pets? I used to have a stick insect but Rupert ate it.'

'Well sort of,' Alice said. 'When I was about your age, I lived in Scotland and my brothers used to go down to the river to catch salmon. I would tag along, watching them, and I used to think of the fish as my pets.'

Lydia frowned. 'Uncle Wolfie has salmon in his shed. They're nothing like Rupert.'

'It was my job to get the roe from them and scoop it into little glass jars that we'd sell in the market.'

'What's roe?'

'The fishes' eggs.'

'What? You'd take them out?'

'Yes, I'd sit with my legs crossed just like you are now, and lie the salmon across my knees and rub the belly from top to bottom. A little bit like petting a dog but pushing down as you go.'

'But fish are scaly!'

'It feels smooth, not slimy like you'd think. And it's so satisfying when the roe slides out.'

'What does it look like?'

'Tiny pink-orange marbles. You can pop them in your mouth and they're delicious. Salty.'

'You eat their babies?' Lydia said, wide-eyed.

Alice smiled. 'Well, I suppose in a way, yes. But also no. It's hard to explain.'

'Why don't you get a dog now you're a grown-up?'

'I don't know. I think it would remind me of my dad always saying no.'

'What about your mum?'

'She died when I was very little.'

Lydia sucked on a strand of her hair. 'My mum's gone away but I think she'll be back soon. Can you push me on the swings?'

Lydia held out a hand. Her slim fingers slotted into Alice's and the sweat of their palms mingled. They walked to the playground and she wondered what kind of image the two of them struck. Could she pass as her mother? A young grandmother? The sun was higher now, casting its slanted rays over the park. Lydia ran to the swings, her bun unravelling in the wind and flying out in greasy streaks behind her. Why had no one told her to wash her hair? What was her father doing?

Each time Alice pushed the rubber tyre, Lydia squealed and coiled her hands around the chains. 'Higher, higher,' she commanded. Alice pushed harder and Lydia's legs kicked in the air in an effort to gain speed. She whooped with pleasure. Back and forth. Back and forth. Alice felt longing spilling out of her. She wanted to spend the whole afternoon with this little girl. Make her shriek with laughter, wait for her at the bottom of the slide, dust dirt from her hands. She knew it was wrong, that she should return the child, but a sudden sense of anarchy took hold. The girl could come to her house. She could feed her. Read her stories. She wouldn't let her out of her sight. Not even for a minute. Why had no one come looking for her?

Lydia jumped down. 'I'm pretty good at the swings.'

'Have you had breakfast?'

'Two slices of toast.'

'That's not enough. Let's get something to eat.'

The house was silent, and that embarrassed her. It was far too big for one person to live in, she saw this clearly now. Lydia ran ahead of her and into the kitchen. Her light foot-steps echoed on the polished concrete floor that Malik had chosen and Alice had always found unpleasant, utilitarian.

'There are fat statues everywhere!' Lydia cried out.

Alice found her cross-legged on the floor stroking the head of a Buddha.

'You can have that one if you want. It's from Nepal.' She opened the fridge. It was almost empty. She poured two glasses of orange juice.

'It's so clean here.'

Alice looked around. The kitchen exhibited no signs of life. No buttered knife left on the side of the sink, no crumbs, no half-drunk mug of coffee, no cookbook left open on the last page it was used. The room was photograph-ready for no reason at all. She went to the cupboard and pulled out a glass jar of macadamia and coconut balls.

'Do you have a nut allergy or anything?'

'Mum says I have a tank for a belly.'

She offered the jar. Lydia stood, took two energy balls and chewed. She continued to pet the head of the Buddha but looked perplexed. Desiccated coconut covered her top lip.

'No good?' Alice asked.

'Where is everyone?'

Alice sagged. 'Who?'

'Your family.' Lydia grimaced. 'I need to pee.'

Alice directed her to the bathroom. In the quiet, she stood at the window to the garden and remembered the morning of the last time Malik had been in the house. She'd rolled over in bed to find his side cold again. He was in the kitchen, banging his fists on the glass. *Damn squirrels are eating the birdfeed again.*

'There's no one upstairs either,' Lydia said. 'Are they all out?'

Alice turned, startled. Lydia looked so small in her kitchen, so out of place. 'Yes,' she said. They were silent for a while, watching the squirrels on the birdfeeder.

'Have you ever seen a baby dragonfly?' Lydia asked.

'No, how do they look?'

'Like aliens! They're born in water and live there till they become dragonflies and then they can zoom into the air like this.' She ran on the spot and furiously flapped her arms.

'That's pretty cool. How they get to live underwater *and* fly.'

'I know.' Lydia's expression was solemn. 'They're special. They must have been very, very good in their past life.' A small scar on her wrist had turned silver next to her tan and she stroked it.

'What counts as good?'

'Being nice to people, including not lying. So if you're like, really good then you've done life well and you don't need another chance at it so you die and then that's it. But if you're bad you come back again to get another chance to be good.'

'Huh,' Alice said. She swallowed. How would she fare by Lydia's rules? 'I think I'd better get you home. Your dad must be worried. Grab your stuff.'

Lydia made a sound like a whinnying horse but gripped Alice's hand tight. Her knuckles were sweet fat knots.

Lydia took a key from her backpack and opened the door. 'Come see my paintings.'

Inside, the air was sour, blinds drawn against the sun. Alice was startled by the sound of a phone ringing. It'd been a long time since she'd heard a landline. 'Should we pick that up?' she asked Lydia just as the ringing stopped.

'Dad was asleep on the couch before. Freddy's at football. Come on, come on, the paintings are in here.'

The kitchen was full of pots-and-pans clutter and gasping plants. Alice touched a honey-sticky spoon that lay face down on a French dictionary. A cream fridge dominated the room, postcards pinned with magnets across its surface, cheerless scenes of a city rooftops, generic sunsets. She resisted the urge to flip them, read of delicacies eaten, weather good or bad. The oven timer blinked 00:00.

'Look,' Lydia said, pointing.

An entire wall was covered with colourful pandas. Their faces were oversized, features stretched and distorted. There was a panda head on a ballerina's body, one in striped pyjamas with butterflies at its feet.

'Wow!' said Alice. 'These are fantastic.'

'Mum says they're advanced for my age.'

As they walked through the room, Alice stumbled on a dog bowl and Lydia caught her arm.

'I'm going to bury the bowl in the garden,' Lydia said, and rushed outside clutching it against her chest.

The door to the living room was open. Inside, the first thing Alice noticed were the two buttons which barely held his shirt together. Curled chest hairs rose and fell in time with each snore. An arm was draped across his face, neck sprinkled with dark moles. She sat on the couch beside him and briefly saw herself on the edge of Malik's hospital bed when they were waiting for results.

On the mantelpiece was a vase filled with dead sun-flowers and a silver-framed photograph of Lydia with a tall, thin boy by her side. They had the same round eyes and defiant chin. The room was small and had the stale air of a place abandoned even though it was full of belongings.

From outside, there came the sound of church bells ringing the hour. She stood up to leave and knocked over a mug on the floor.

The man startled awake and rubbed his eyes. His skin was drawn tight across his jaw and his cheekbones were angular, sharp. He jumped up when he saw Alice.

'This must look weird,' she said. 'I'm Alice. I live across the park.'

'Why are you here?' He squinted at her. 'I've seen you. You're the one who naps under the tree in the mornings.'

She smiled. 'I brought your daughter home. She ran away to the swings.'

He rubbed his eyes again and thanked her. 'I didn't get a good night's sleep. She must have slipped out when I nodded off.' He extended a hand. The skin felt rough but his grip was firm. 'Luca,' he said. 'Lydia's very upset. Our dog died yesterday.' He looked down, shrugged and quickly buttoned up his shirt.

'She told me. She's outside burying his dog bowl.'

'Good grief.' He shook his head. 'She thinks it's my fault.'

'Your daughter's quite the charmer.'

Luca returned her smile, exposing rows of white crooked teeth. Alice figured he wasn't yet in his forties. Handsome, with a good mop of hair.

He gestured at the room. 'It's chaos in here, I know. My wife left, my son won't speak to me because he thinks it's my fault, and now the damn dog is dead.'

Alice nodded. 'If I boil my eggs for too long in the morning then my day can turn to ribbons.'

He stared at her for a moment. 'It's been weeks and I'm still not on top of all the washing.'

'My husband had cirrhosis of the liver. I haven't cleared out the bathroom cabinet yet. All his medicines are there in an orderly row. The dates and his name on the labels are comforting. I don't know why.'

'I'm so sorry. I can't even imagine.' He paused. 'Would you like some coffee, maybe? I get the beans sent over from Italy – a place near where I grew up.'

The kitchen blinds clattered as he raised them. The room filled with late-morning light. It bounced off the white tiles and made the disarray around them seem softer. Outside, Lydia was digging in the earth with a wooden spoon. Luca flicked the kettle on and ran a hand through his hair. The black curls bounced back.

'That's not even our garden she's digging in,' he said, gesturing at Lydia. 'It belongs to our neighbour.' He sighed and shook his head. 'I have no idea how she's really doing. About her mum, I mean. She says the most adult stuff.'

'Listening to her is enough right now. She needs you.'

Alice went to the oven, checked her watch, and fiddled with the buttons until they reached the correct time. She stood by the window. Lydia was curtseying before a mound of soil she'd displaced from a flower bed. Behind her was a bayberry bush, the bright blue of the sky and the proud row of beech trees which lined the edges of the park. Beyond them was Alice's house. The park looked so different from this side. She could be in another place entirely.

Luca moved between the breakfast counter and the sink in a harmony of scraping and stacking dishes. He poured the coffee into heavy ceramic mugs. She took a sip. It was strong. Black and reviving.

'Are you hungry?' he asked. 'I could make some eggs. I find cooking helps.'

She smiled and sat down at the counter. He cracked the eggs, four, five, six, and whisked them with whole milk, chatting idly about his dairy supplier at the deli. Alice tuned into the clang of the tin whisk against the glass bowl. Metallic and melodic. A sound so similar to the meditation bells, but instead of time slowing down, losing its momentum, it gained speed. Like a wind-up key in the back of a child's toy, turning and turning until it was ready to scuttle away.

September

Let Us Rejoice!

'Why is she wearing that for her second wedding?' someone behind Mona whispered. The question lingered in the air, polluting it like cigarette smoke. Mona turned in her seat as her distant cousin negotiated her hips down the aisle. The offending dress was fussy with an unforgiving tightness to it – very fitting, she thought, for a forty-year-old woman who wished she were thirty. The rest of the wedding guests looked ordinary enough, though there were too many lumpy women with sour mouths. Who were they all, anyway?

The room was pearl-white, and purple taffeta bows had been tied across the backs of the chairs. Mona looked down at her sandals. 'They're still there,' she murmured. 'These are my feet. One, two, three, four, five, six, seven, eight, nine, ten toes on the floor of – is this an atrium?' She turned to Wolfie. 'Why aren't we in a synagogue? Is the groom a goy?'

'Mona, shush. People can hear you,' he whispered. 'The groom converted but they decided not to marry in a synagogue. You've met him before. You find him pleasant enough, a bit nebbish, though – clearly a man who works in computers. Actually, you told him that at Shabbas dinner once. It was pretty funny.'

'Wolfie! Did I say that?'

'Well it was what everyone was thinking, darling.' He removed his new glasses and polished the lenses with his suit sleeve before settling them back on the end of his nose.

'What's that young woman doing up there?' Mona asked.

'It's Rabbi Ellensen. She took over last year when Rabbi Rubenstein retired. Actually, she came to dinner once but you weren't feeling very well that day. She was going to say a blessing at our anniversary celebrations.'

'What! A woman can't be a rabbi. That's meshuggina!'

'I heard the Stevenses were married by a female rabbi last year. It's some new trend the kids are into.'

'Will you two please be quiet!' a woman hissed from the row behind.

'Blessed are you who come in the name of Adonai,' the rabbi said. 'Marriage, which creates a link between all past generations and all future generations, is much more than a private milestone for the couple, it's a historic and momentous event for the community at large. So it is with much joy that I stand today beneath this beautifully decorated chuppah, which we remember represents the couple's new home, the very foundation of the Jewish family.'

The woman in front shifted and her elaborate hat blocked Mona's view of the rabbi. Inside its netting several pieces of plastic fruit knocked into each other. She was reminded of something but she couldn't quite grasp what. Breakfast? She tried to pluck a banana from the hat but the woman spun round and glared at her.

'Shhh,' Mona said.

Through the window, people dressed in black darted back and forth clutching chairs and trussed-up table centrepieces. The flowers left much to be desired.

'The Torah tells us: love your fellow as yourself,' the rabbi said.

Mona pulled at the two clips which clung to Wolfie's wispy strands. 'Your yarmulke isn't straight,' she murmured. She shifted it to the centre of his bald spot and brushed the dandruff from his shoulders. 'Sixty-five years of marriage.'

'Yes, my love.'

Wolfie took her loose-skinned hand in his and played with the gold rings that just about managed to stay on her fingers. She returned his squeeze and smiled.

There she was, eighteen, with a stomach full of butterflies and half of the bagel Wolfie sent over to Patrice's before the ceremony. It was still rationing time, so he must have got the cream cheese on the black market. Very sly. Oh and those curlers! How Patrice spent ages pulling them out and hairspraying each section. The dress she made herself. Stiff white fabric which used up all her coupons. Simple and modest, a sweetheart neckline with long sleeves. No embroidery, or girlish embellishment, none of this schmutter on today's bride. Her real thrill came from wearing lipstick for the first time. It was that soft wash of pink which made her feel she was finally an adult, finally free of her foster family. And Wolfie, how handsome he looked! All that thick dark hair. He'd borrowed the suit from Monty but you could never have guessed – it had been tailored to perfection. There was no money for fresh flowers, but at the synagogue he was waiting for her with a single white rose.

'So now,' the rabbi said, 'as the bride circles the groom three times, she creates an invisible wall around her husband into which she will step to the exclusion of all others.'

Mona followed the words as the couple made their declaration to one another, her tongue wrapping around familiar syllables. 'Harei at mekudeshet li b'tabaat zu k'dat Moshe v'Yisrael.' Be consecrated to me, with this ring, according to the religion and tradition of Moses and Israel. The bride and groom tripped over the words. Some nervousness was understandable, though – she and

Patrice had a little nip from a bottle of sherry before her and Wolfie's ceremony.

The rabbi placed a cloth-covered glass on the ground. 'There are many stories behind this tradition,' she continued. 'But most important is how it reminds us that love is fragile and must be protected. The promises made by these two people today are as irrevocable as the broken glass. Let us remember the teaching in Berakhot: where there is rejoicing, there should be trembling.'

The groom stomped on the bundle and the crunch elicited a resounding 'Mazel tov!' from the wedding guests. The bride and groom kissed. They seemed to knock teeth. Mona had never seen a couple less enamoured with each other.

A bridesmaid darted out from the front row and suddenly an ethereal voice floated down the aisle along with husband and wife. Mona listened to the words. She *knew* them. Softly, she sang along.

'Wolfie, do you hear this? What a strange song to choose.'

'Yes, darling. It's Joni. Your favourite. I took you to her concert once. I had to pull double shifts at the deli for two weeks to pay for the tickets.'

'Oh I did? We did?'

'Yes, you wore your hair in thick braids that night and a floaty dress. You looked like an angel.'

*

An overweight and overwrought wedding planner herded the guests into the hotel's medium-sized reception room. To each person she said, 'Come on now, come on. The next wedding is in two hours.' Mona wished she'd stop prodding her back. The bustle was crushing and she tightened her grip on Wolfie's hand, using the other to hold on to his elbow. 'Don't leave me on my own,' she said. He smiled and mouthed, 'Not a chance.'

Corks popped and waiters weaved through the crowd. Eager hands groped for whatever happened to be laid across the silver trays, but Mona didn't have much appetite for such chazerai food.

Wolfie led her to a group which had gathered around a middle-aged woman in a puffy mint-green dress. Her hair was piled high on her head and white feathers poked out from the nest. The women surrounding her were clucking and cooing. Mona recognized Wolfie's look of frustration when he couldn't get a word in – just like a child when you took away their dummy. She tuned into the conversation.

'Mazel tov! You look absolutely resplendent in that green. Resplendent. You must be so proud. Your daughter looks beautiful. What a couple.'

'Oh, very proud. Very proud indeed. And you – you look great. Did you change your hair colour?'

'I did! Chestnut. It's chestnut.'

'Well it suits you. Warms up your skin tone.'

'Oh thank you. I have to say, I did *not* expect to see Rachel here.'

'I'm afraid that was my daughter's decision. But I suppose we couldn't very well not invite her. Family is family.'

'Her boy turned out strange, didn't he?'

'Mona and I would like to offer our heartfelt congratulations on such a joyous occasion,' Wolfie finally said, embracing the woman in the green dress. The others drifted away.

'Darling Mona!' the woman replied. 'It's been years. My God, look at you. You need to eat more! Isn't Wolfie feeding you?'

Mona looked down at her body. 'This isn't my dress,' she said. 'It's horrible! Who would wear a brown dress?'

'You look lovely,' Wolfie said. 'I bought that dress for you.'

'Why would you do that to me?'

'It's gorgeous,' the woman said. 'You always manage to look so willowy for your age, although you really *must* eat more.'

'I've seen you gobbling up the fish balls,' Mona said. 'There are other people who like them, you know.'

Mona spotted the groom pressed up against the paisley wallpaper, trying to look anonymous. The purple flower in his buttonhole drooped and he was perspiring at the temples. A narrow-shouldered man was never attractive, no matter how expensive a suit you put him in. She walked over.

'Thank you for coming, Mona,' he said. 'It's so lovely to see you. You look wonderful as usual.'

'Why did you marry her of all people?'

He coughed and ran a hand through his hair. 'She's just – she's just so familiar.'

'Oy gevalt. What a thing to say.'

'I know.'

'There's a secret to being happily married... There's. Oh. I.'

The groom smiled at her. 'This is wedding number two – I could use some advice.'

'You're a good boy. I see that. I'm very tired.'

'Me too. These things are exhausting.'

'A hand on the knee. Arm around her shoulder. Let her know you always want to be near her. That she's always on your mind. You'll have a long and happy marriage. Like me.'

'That's lovely, Mona.'

'Where's Wolfie?' she asked. 'Where is he? Where is he?'

'He's just over there. Can you see? He's waving.'

'Can I have the bride's family first?' the photographer asked. 'Please move away from the chuppah and out into the gardens.'

Mona was swept along as people put down their bucks' fizzes and trickled out of the reception room to gather in front of the rose garden.

'Arrange yourselves in height order for me,' the photographer said. 'Has anyone seen the wedding planner? I need her help.'

Mona spied a woman hiding behind the hydrangeas with a cigarette.

'Those with children, can you keep an eye on them?' the photographer continued. 'No running around. Can we have the little ones in a row in the front, please?'

'Oy, kids. You're driving me crazy. Stop fussing with the flowers.'

'But, Nana, she has more pink than me.'

'Well you have more purple, bubala.'

'That's not the same!'

'Kids, we're doing my photos now. Can you please behave for one minute?'

'Everybody back up a little bit,' the photographer said. 'A little bit more. Great, now look at me, please, and smile. Look at me. Kids, I mean at me, not at your mummy.'

'Shall I tilt my head to the left or the right? What's more flattering?'

'Nothing will improve it, dear,' Mona said.

'Either way is just lovely, madam.'

'Mona? Don't wander off. You've got to be in the picture.'

'Oh Christ, what does she think she's doing?'

'Can we get this done before we die of starvation?'

'Wolfie, how *is* Mona?'

'Compared to what?'

'Compared to the last time I saw her.'

'Well, older probably. Perhaps you'd like to ask her yourself?'

'Why are they talking about me like I'm not here?' she asked Wolfie. He looked very tired.

'Oy, they're a bunch of drecks. Just smile, my darling, and keep your hands by your sides,' he replied. 'We'll be done soon and then we can sit down again.'

'Good. My feet hurt,' she said.

'OK, OK. Are we all here? Let's go. Everybody ready?'

'No, wait – can you please make sure my hair looks tidy?'

'It's perfect.'

'Oh my gosh, guys, you look incredible. You'll remember this day for the rest of your lives. Everybody say "Mazel tov!"'

'Mazel tov!'

'Got it. '

'We're done?'

'You're done! Beautiful. What a beautiful bunch.'

'OK, everybody gai aveck.'

'Let's go – I'm starving.'

'I hope the main isn't cod. It's been wretched cod at every wedding this summer.'

Mona understood their need for sustenance. It could take a lot out of you to wear a false smile for so long.

'Why are there so many lights while we're eating, Wolfie?' Mona asked. 'Look! There's one on my shoe. My dress!' She tried to brush it off but it wouldn't budge.

'It's from a disco ball, darling. Look up. Like the seventies, when you loved to go dancing. I never moved my hips right and other men would come and ask if you wanted a *real* dance partner. Oy, I hated it. You always looked good in gold sequins, though. Matched your hair.'

'Yes, yes, Wolfie, I remember. The light's making it very hard to see what I'm eating. Maybe that's a good thing.'

'Mona!' her neighbour admonished. 'You're terrible – but you have a point. Is it some kind of sponge?'

'It looks like something we ate during the war,' Wolfie said. 'You know, a supposedly kosher friend of mine told me the other day that he eats abstract meat. When I asked what that was exactly he said, "Really overprocessed ham, the worst kind. So different from its original form that it can only be defined as an abstract representation of pig."'

Everyone laughed but Mona was sure she'd heard that one a hundred times.

'I don't like this dark,' she whispered in Wolfie's ear. He squeezed her knee. It was nice. She turned her attention to the band onstage. The singer was much too tall and thin but her dress had beautiful wide sleeves that fanned out as she raised her arms. Mona wanted to get up and touch them but she liked the gentle weight of Wolfie's hand on her leg. It was good to be a wife. She plucked a petal from the flower arrangement and stroked its smooth surface. There were no flowers at the pub where they had their wedding party. Just the single white rose pinned to her dress. Not many people either, but once the room filled with dancing and laughing and toasts to the happy couple, it made her feel like she had the blessing of the whole East End. Monty gave a marvellous best man's speech. They should really send him a special card to say thank you for all his hard work. And Wolfie did wonders with the food. Everyone ate their fill and went home with full bellies. So, in the end, it was a relief her foster parents never showed up. A wedding was no place for misery guts.

'These bands cost an absolute fortune,' someone said. 'Last year, at Cousin Danny's, they had a DJ and I thought it was just as good.'

'Nothing beats live music,' Wolfie said. 'That's how you know it's a real celebration. Isn't that right, my love?'

The band finished their warm-up and the opening bars of 'Hava Nagila' leaped and plunged through the air. She set down her glass of orange juice and rose from the table, the others following her lead. Soon the whole party made its way to the dance floor, hands clasped in front of chests, clapping in time to the old beat.

The men gathered to one side of the room, the women to the other. Each word of the blessing, each movement of the dance she knew. She remembered. She sang along in a bright clear tone.

Hava nagila, hava nagila, hava nagila
Ve-nisma-cha, ve-nisma-cha
Hava na-ranana, hava na-ranana, hava na-ranana
Ve-nisma-cha, ve-nisma cha.

The violins' sweeping refrain rose above the piano. Onstage, the singer was loud and confident as she chased the cello's playful melody. Mona's own singing voice was good, she knew. Did she still sing for the synagogue choir? She'd ask Wolfie about that one. There he was, at the other end of the crowd. So handsome in his navy blue suit. She really was a lucky girl. The band picked up speed and so did the clapping. The rest of the wedding guests added their own misguided inflections to the words. They linked hands and formed circles like atom rings, the bride and groom the nucleus.

Wolfie had stepped back from the crowd. His knees must be hurting. She pulled away from the women and joined him at the side of the dance floor where he was talking to a young man.

'Spectacular, isn't it?' Wolfie was saying. He took Mona's arm. 'You should be flying around with them. It's custom for everyone to dance, Jewish or not.'

'I can't do it properly.'

'Let your feet find the way. The rest of you will follow. Life's too short to be self-conscious.'

'I can't get into it. A wedding's nothing more than expensive ritual, don't you think? We just go through the motions, doing what everyone expects of us…'

'How can you say that?' Wolfie replied, wagging a finger. 'Rituals remind us we're connected to each other – to history. We need to honour them. And weddings can be beautiful without being expensive. I should know; we did ours on a shoestring.'

The man smiled. 'How long have you two been married?'

'Sixty-five years. We were both Kindertransport children. I came from Germany and Mona from Austria. We met at a dance in east London, and three months later I made her my wife.'

'Jesus! What's the secret?'

'We find simple ways to say complicated things to each other, don't we, Mona? I'd spend sixty-five more years with you if this body of mine would hold out.'

'How many years?' she asked. 'You're full of nonsense.'

Wolfie pulled her closer.

'Why are you looking at me like that?' she asked the man. 'It's not polite.'

'I think I will join in with the dancing after all. Nice to meet you both. Excuse me.'

'Take no notice of him, darling,' Wolfie said. 'Shall we get back out there? Show the young ones we've still got it?'

She nodded. The clapping had intensified. In the women's corner, the bride was hoisted on to a wooden chair by two strapping men and lifted into the air. With a nervous smile, she gripped its sides as they moved her closer to her new husband. He was waving a white hanky. The bride gingerly reached out and took hold of one corner. The crowd whooped their approval.

How many bat and bar mitzvahs, how many weddings, how many milestones had she celebrated? She could remember Israel, the year after Ester died. The first time she'd been on a plane. The image was right there – Masada, Tel Aviv, then Jerusalem, the heat and crush of people, and who did it belong to, and who did she belong to?

Hands pulled her along, widening the circle, and each woman crossed right leg over left leg as they orbited the bride and groom, faster and faster, knees rising higher and higher in time to the jagged violins. It was joy, it was joy, the music of Israel. How it whirred and whirred.

Wolfie held open the cab door for his wife and waited as she concertinaed her body into the space. Inside, they both leaned back into the leather seats, exhausted. The low hum of the resting engine turned into a rush and soon the dark suburban sky gave way to an onslaught of city lights.

'Where are we going?' Mona asked. Shadows had deepened beneath her eyes.

'Home, my love,' he said. 'We're going home.'

Rosary beads hung from the rear-view mirror and swayed back and forth at every stop and start. Wolfie stared at the passing scenery, the gaudy colours and windows full of schmutter. Even after so many decades in London, the West End's rowdy streets bemused him. Every available inch of space sprouting a building, the same shops and fast-food chains punctuating each corner. He couldn't understand the desire to extend skywards. Too much concrete and brick; too little sense of community. He never thought of it as the city centre – Victoria Park was his hub.

They passed a gym, rows of men and women running on treadmills. What energy was driving them so late at night? What were they running from?

The cab stopped in traffic outside a block of luxury glass-walled flats. In daylight they must look shimmering, but at night they absorbed the neon glow of shop signs. How did anyone sleep in all that brightness, the twenty-four-hour-ness of it? He watched an empty escalator, waiting to deliver someone up or down, or nowhere really, in the end.

Drunken folk tripped out of pubs and restaurants and overwhelmed the pavements with their urgency. A torrent of people coming and going, smoking and shouting. They boarded buses, flagged black cabs. A group of young women with neck tattoos and glassy eyes crossed the street, paying no heed to the flow of traffic. He turned to comment on them to Mona but she was asleep. It had been a long day for her – she'd done well. He opened the window. Yells and guffaws mingled with the greasy scent of fried onions.

'Do you want the air con on, sir?' the driver asked.

'Pardon?' His ears were still ringing with music.

'The air conditioning, sir.'

'No, no, thank you. Nice to have a bit of a breeze.'

The cab turned into a quiet, tree-lined neighbourhood. The golden orbs of old-fashioned street lamps made a carpet of light on the pavement. Crisp, cool air rushed in. Everything here felt different, somehow – clearer. The Georgian town houses had grand sash windows, white porticos, and sleek sports cars parked outside. Amazing how quickly the city could reveal another side of her personality.

They pulled into a modest driveway, gravel sounding its protest beneath the wheels. The headlights swept across the building in front of them. Ivy trailed from its windows. Wolfie took a long look at Mona. Her head had sunk forward, her body slumped, but she looked peaceful all the same. Little snuffling noises escaped her open mouth. His bones ached. He longed to curl around her.

The cab stopped and the driver swivelled his head.

'I'll just be a moment,' Wolfie said. He unbuckled Mona's seat belt and softly brushed her cheek. 'Wake up, my darling, we're here.'

Mona yawned and blinked a few times. She looked at Wolfie and then stared out of the window. 'Am I drunk?' she asked.

'No no, my love. You've been asleep.'

His knees clicked as he manoeuvred himself out of the cab. He opened the door for his wife. She took his outstretched hand and they walked towards the main entrance together, his arm encircling her waist. A breeze moved through the laburnums that bordered the path. Each step felt heavy.

A young carer was waiting in the doorway, a light behind her. 'You lovebirds are always breaking curfew,' she teased. 'We were expecting her back much earlier. How was the wedding, Mona?'

'Oh I don't know. It was a wedding.'

Wolfie kissed her hands, her papery cheeks and then her dry lips. There was nothing to do but tell her he loved her and then leave.

'Where's he going?' Mona asked.

Wolfie turned. The carer had put her arm around Mona's shoulders and was guiding her inside. He kept walking.

'Where's he going?' she repeated with more urgency.

Wolfie, his back to the building now, paused and flinched before opening the car door and edging into his seat. The leather creaked.

'On to Victoria Park now, sir?' the driver asked.

Wolfie nodded and kept his gaze fixed forward.

Acknowledgements

A book is the very definition of a community project. This one is the summation of encouragement, generosity, and the discerning eyes of family and friends to whom I give heartfelt thanks, and a large gang of brilliant readers and writers including a heroic group of UEA and Goldsmiths alumni, with extra gratitude to Emily Ruth Ford – who goes the extra mile and then some.

I owe a special thanks to my fellow students and faculty at Bath Spa University, where the genesis of this book took place – particularly to Gavin Cologne-Brookes and Samantha Harvey for their wisdom and emphatic honesty, and to Natasha Randall and Jane Saotome for becoming my London writing family.

Thank you to the entire team at Allen and Unwin, especially Kate Ballard, whose skills helped this book realize itself and whose amicability made that process infinitely less painful than it should have been, and to Sarah-Jane Forder who whipped my words into their slickest shape.

To my agent, Seren Adams, who could see the vision and helped me run with it. You have been the perfect ally, thank you.

And to AO, for everything, always.